D0962131

THE CHOICE

The Virtual War Chronologs
by Gloria Skurzynski

Virtual War [Book 1]

The Clones [Book 2]

The Revolt [Book 3]

The Choice [Book 4]

THE VIRTUAL WAR CHRONOLOGS

THE CHOICE

BOOK 4

GLORIA SKURZYNSKI

ATHENEUM BOOKS FOR YOUNG READERS
NEW YORK LONDON TORONTO SYDNEY

Atheneum Books for Young Readers
An imprint of Simon & Schuster Children's Publishing Division
1230 Avenue of the Americas
New York, New York 10020
Book design by Russell Gordon
The text of this book is set in Aldine 401, Rant, and Trade Gothic.
Manufactured in the United States of America
First Edition
2 4 6 8 10 9 7 5 3 1
Library of Congress Cataloging-in-Publication Data
Skurzynski, Gloria.
The choice / Gloria Skurzynski.
p. cm. — (The virtual war chronologs ; 4)
Summary: Tired and disillusioned, Corgan tries living a more peaceful life on
Nuku Hiva, but soon must confront his nemesis, Brigand, for the last time.
ISBN-13: 978-0-689-84267-2
ISBN-10: 0-689-84267-8
[1. Science fiction.] I. Title II. Series: Skurzynski, Gloria. Virtual war
chronologs ; bk. 4.
PZ7.S6287Cho 2006
[Fic]—dc22
2005025163

For my five fabulous daughters—
Serena, Jan, Joni, Lanie, and
Lauren

THE CHOICE

THE CHOICE

One

The sky was vast. Forty-five minutes of darkness followed forty-five minutes of light as Corgan circled Earth one more time. Before the next orbit, and while the others were still asleep, he needed to make his decision.

The choice was his—they knew that, he'd told them that. Cyborg's silence didn't matter, Sharla's wishes didn't matter, and neither did Ananda's tears.

Flying the spacecraft was easy for Corgan. Choosing *where* to go was infinitely harder. The *Prometheus* could make it all the way to Mars, if he chose Mars, but it would take two months to get there and would use up a huge amount of fuel. Why waste time and energy to arrive on a planet that might be as dead as the colonists who'd once tried to settle it? Those colonists had flown on a rocket ship to Mars in 2018, sixty-four years ago, but no one on Earth had heard from them since their landing. *If* they ever landed.

Corgan touched the controls to set the numbers that would keep the *Prometheus* circumnavigating Earth. Then, cautiously, he turned to look at his three passengers: Cyborg, the closest friend he'd ever had; Ananda, whose heart he'd just broken; and Sharla, who kept on breaking Corgan's heart. They stayed asleep, all three of them. Ananda and Cyborg lay together on the flight deck, her tearstained face pressed against his shoulder. Sharla slumped forward in one of the deck seats, her head resting on her arms as though she'd grown tired looking through the window—or port, as Cyborg kept reminding them to call the wraparound pane that circled the top deck of the *Prometheus*.

Corgan turned his back on them because he had to decide, and if he didn't look at them, deciding would be easier. He knew well enough what each of them wanted. Ananda was desperate to return to the space station, but Corgan couldn't go back there because he'd stolen something valuable from the three people who lived on the station. Sharla and Cyborg wanted to go back to the Florida domed city, where Brigand ruled—Brigand, Cyborg's clone-twin and Corgan's worst enemy, who would happily destroy Corgan as soon as he saw him.

He'd grown weary of all the battles and fears and controversy he'd lived through in the past year. He felt tired, disillusioned, used by everyone and without ever getting much back. He wanted to feel good again, to be happy once more, like he'd been those six great months after he won the Virtual War. Remembering, letting his mind fill with scenes of the island, Corgan could almost feel the clean air and the surf and the growing trees that gave fruit as well as shade. The islands were the one and only place on Earth where a person could live in complete freedom from contamination. Far outside the domed cities, the Isles of Hiva were a world where sun warmed your skin and moonlight shone pure into your eyes, instead of being filtered to dullness through domeglass. On Nuku Hiva he used to run on the beach with Sharla, watching her golden hair turn even brighter gold in the sunlight. Once, he danced with her on the beach—but only that one time—when he thought she might love him. Maybe Sharla remembered it too, and all those memories would bring them closer once again, if they returned to the island.

He studied the holographic control panels, the ones he'd installed by himself back in the Florida domed city. Where did the *Prometheus* happen to be flying right then, right that split second? He wasn't sure because navigation was his weakest skill, but it seemed that they were high above the South American continent.

Okay, he said to himself, *you know where you want to go, so do it—lift up your hand and change direction.* According to the holographic sphere of Earth, he was in the southern hemisphere. Focusing intently, he reached for the transparent touch screen. He would need to pilot the ship from a latitude of 26° south to 9° south, from a longitude of 48° west to 139° west.

Stay asleep, he silently urged the other three. *Don't wake up and find out what I'm doing.* The change of course as the *Prometheus* turned in the sky was so gentle that they slept undisturbed. Heading in its new direction, softly, quietly, the *Prometheus* felt almost becalmed—Corgan had to fight to keep *himself* awake. He hadn't slept for nearly two days, or to be exact, for forty-two hours, thirty-seven minutes, and seventeen and a quarter seconds. Funny how his time-splitting ability kept on functioning even when he felt groggy.

Wake up! he commanded himself. *Stay alert!* He didn't worry about the *Prometheus* crashing—Thebos had designed it to avoid sudden, dangerous impacts—but if Corgan dozed off, the spaceship could go wandering all over the Pacific

Ocean far beneath them. He bit the back of his hand, not hard enough to draw blood, but with just enough pain to keep himself sharp.

After two hours of biting his knuckles he noticed Sharla lift her head slowly, raising her hand to push her hair away from her cheek. Once, that hair had been long and flowing, but now it was cropped shorter than she liked it, barely brushing her neck. What a contrast the two girls were: Sharla all ivory and gold, with wide blue eyes; Ananda a jewel of dark amber with eyes coffee brown, her hair black and shiny. Both were beautiful, Corgan thought.

As Sharla peered sleepily through the port, she caught sight of Corgan's reflection in its pane. He put a finger to his lips to signal her to stay silent. Would she? Sharla didn't react too well to orders from anyone.

"Where are we?" she mouthed.

Silently he pointed to the Earth hologram, his hand hovering over the emptiness of the ocean.

This time she whispered her question. "Where are we going?"

To the place where we were happy. He didn't say anything out loud; he just shook his head a little, gesturing toward Cyborg and Ananda.

They woke up anyway. Like Sharla, they stared through the port, curious about where Corgan had brought them. Just as Cyborg was about to speak, Corgan held up his hand and said, "Before you ask me anything, I want to say something to Ananda. I know how awful you feel about the dog, Ananda, and I want to say I'm really sorry. *Really* sorry. I'm telling you the truth when I say that I had to leave Demi up there on the space station to honor the deal I made with the Driscolls. For 'one of the girls' to stay with them."

"You already told us that, Corgan," Cyborg said.

"But I have to say it again until Ananda finally understands. It was the only way they'd let us use the Locker, and we *had* to use the Locker. So I dealt with it. In my mind I classified Demi as 'one of the girls.'"

"She *is* a girl!" Ananda cried, those dark eyes glistening with tears again. "To you she's just a dog, but to me she's my beloved friend that I was closer to than any human in the world after I lost my parents and grandparents. She was my *family*. I love her as much as I love Cyborg."

"Thanks a lot," Cyborg muttered.

Ananda whirled on him. "I know you don't understand it. No one understands. Now that I'll never see Demi again, it'll take me a while to get over the hurt."

"Hey, listen!" Corgan cried. "I did the best I could in a bad situation. I gave them my pledge, and that's got to count for something." The words came rushing out of his mouth as he tried to justify his actions, to himself as much as to Ananda. "I did what I promised, and it may not have been a perfect execution, but it saved you or Sharla from a pretty bad life, Ananda. If you want to stay mad at me, that's your choice."

"*You're* the one who's making all the choices, Corgan," Cyborg broke in. "We don't even know where you're taking us."

"You'll figure it out in a few minutes," Corgan replied tensely. At least he wasn't fatigued anymore—defending himself had fired him up. Now he felt alert and in command.

Just before they broke through the cloud cover, Corgan

set the *Prometheus* to hover slowly at five kilometers altitude, and soon afterward at four, because that's where the clouds began to thin and they could see small patches of ocean. Curious like the others, Corgan peered through the port to discover what lay beneath them. He saw that he was right where he wanted to be. "Strap yourselves in," he told them. "We'll be landing soon."

As the *Prometheus* descended slowly, they could see the whole chain of islands stretched across the ocean, looking like a handful of rocks thrown randomly onto a blue carpet. The spaceship dropped lower in altitude, making the islands appear larger.

"Nuku Hiva," Cyborg said.

"Nuku Hiva," Sharla agreed.

"What's Nuku Hiva?" Ananda asked, peering through the port.

Not answering, Corgan glanced at Sharla and Cyborg to check their reactions, but they looked neither surprised nor particularly pleased.

"Is this the island where . . . ?" Ananda began.

"The island Corgan chose as his reward after winning the Virtual War," Cyborg answered.

"Well, if you won't go back to the space station, Corgan, why can't we just fly back to Florida?" Ananda demanded.

Corgan was about to tell her where she could go, but he cut it off in time. *Do not start out with conflict,* he cautioned himself. Instead he would work toward what was calm and good, and maybe create a whole new life where all of them could bury their hurts and blame and jealousies and bond into tight friendship once again.

"The Isles of Hiva are the only uncontaminated place on Earth," Sharla told Ananda. "Good choice, Corgan."

"Thanks." He hadn't expected approval from anyone, especially Sharla, but he couldn't soak it up right then because he had to land the spacecraft. At one kilometer above Earth the whole island had become visible, a lush, tropical paradise with waves rushing the shores and then sweeping back as though gathering energy for another dash forward. Corgan maneuvered the *Prometheus* toward the concrete landing pad, then suddenly slammed the controls into hover as two figures ran out from beneath the trees. Staring up in amazement, the two people shaded their eyes and bent back to get a better look. Corgan could imagine their bewilderment, since they'd be the first beings on the entire planet Earth ever to see this particular spacecraft land on solid ground.

"That's Delphine down there," Corgan said.

"Who's that with her?" Cyborg asked.

A husky boy, or man, or something in between, was running fast across the sand toward the landing pad. His skin was brown, and his hair looked black and very thick, even from forty meters up. "I guess he's the guy who came to herd the cows after I left," Corgan answered.

"He's kind of cute," Sharla murmured.

On the ground Delphine hurried to catch up to the boy, who'd reached the landing area before she did.

"Hey, he's right in the middle of the pad," Corgan cried. "He needs to move, or we'll land on top of his head."

Delphine must have realized that—she yanked the boy backward. Both of them looked worried, unsure who might be in this strange, saucer-shaped vehicle touching down on their island, but when Sharla pressed her face against the port and waved, Delphine recognized her and began to jump up and down eagerly, her face lighting with pleasure.

Cyborg waved too, with his good hand, and so did Corgan, but then he warned his passengers, "This is the first time I've ever brought down this baby. I hope it won't bounce or—"

"Or crash," Cyborg said.

"Yeah, so you better hang on to something."

The landing couldn't have been smoother. Maybe a soft landing was a good omen, Corgan hoped. Maybe life would be a little smoother too, here on Nuku Hiva.

Two

Corgan slid down the side of the *Prometheus* and landed in the welcoming arms of Delphine. It was okay to be smothered by her hugs, but he squeezed his eyes tight when she kissed his cheek once, twice, three times. From him she moved to Cyborg, crying, "I can't believe it! You're all grown up, and it was just a few months ago that you were a little boy!" Cyborg got even more kisses than Corgan had, and then it was Sharla's turn for hugs. When Delphine reached Ananda, she asked, "Who's this?"

"That's Ananda," Corgan answered. "Who's that?"

"This is Royal," Delphine answered, smiling widely. "Royal is descended from a Polynesian prince."

Royal bent his head a little in acknowledgment. Corgan didn't know what a Polynesian prince was, but it sounded impressive. And Royal was impressive—husky and muscular, he looked like he could wrestle a wild boar to the ground and spear it with its own tusks. "My great-grandfather was a prince," Royal said. "I'm just a cowherd."

Surprised, Ananda told him, "But you look really brave."

"*Cowherd!* Not coward," Corgan corrected her. "Meaning he takes care of cows, like I did when I lived here. I guess you took over my job, Royal," Corgan said. "And Ananda got my other job—if the Virtual War gets fought again, she'll do the fighting." *Which means, face it, I'm out of work,* Corgan thought.

Still delighted, Delphine said, "It'll take hours for all of us to learn everything about one another, and I can't wait to begin, but right now I want to know about this amazing . . . *thing* . . . you just flew in to land on our island. Whose is it? Where did it come from? How does it work?" She ran the palms of her hands over the smooth sides of the spaceship, which were just as shiny and clean as they'd been at the beginning of their voyage from the Flor-DC. No space debris had scarred the hull or pitted the smooth outside of the wraparound panes. Instead of looking like it had just landed, the *Prometheus* looked ready to take off.

"This is a zero-gravity control spacecraft," Corgan began.

Cyborg broke in with, "Designed by an old man who's the last living genius rocket scientist."

Sharla joined with, "You really need to see the inside, Delphine. It's incredible. . . ." Then she paused to take a closer look at Delphine, who'd grown noticeably heavier since they'd last seen her. "Uh . . . or maybe not. The entry is way up there on top."

"Do it this way," Royal instructed. "Sharla—that's your name, right? You climb up, then reach down to grab Delphine's hand when we boost her." Royal knelt, lowering his hands and lacing his fingers together. "Stick your left foot in here, Delphine, and Corgan, do this with your hands and lift up her right foot."

Corgan did what Royal told him to, the two of them heaving in unison to hoist Delphine toward the top of the ship, where Sharla pulled her into the *Prometheus*. The others followed.

Inside, Delphine turned around in wonderment. This woman was a biologist and a geneticist, Corgan knew, but he was surprised at how many intelligent questions she asked about the mechanics of zero-gravity flight. She peered at the holographic control panels, wanting Corgan to demonstrate them. She studied the Earth hologram, touching the position of Nuku Hiva in the central Pacific. She walked all the way around the circular control deck to examine everything. Even though she acted a little . . . *gushy* sometimes, Delphine was one smart lady, the smartest woman Corgan had ever met. And Thebos was the smartest man. What a pair they'd make! Except that Thebos was ninety-one and Delphine was . . . maybe half that? Corgan didn't know.

Royal, who followed Delphine, paused longest in front of the Locker. Touching it cautiously as Cyborg told how it had stopped his aging, he seemed surprised that such a makeshift piece of equipment would be standing inside the sleek, technically complex spaceship.

At last Delphine said, "Let's go, then. Getting out of the *Prometheus* ought to be easier for me than getting in, since gravity will be on my side this time. I want to come back sometime real soon, Corgan, and check the programming of the flight patterns more systematically, and I'd particularly like to hear about the Locker's electronics. But now I'm going back to the lab to cook up a feast. Okay with you guys?"

Even before they answered, she went on, "What a celebration we'll have! Royal, will you slay a fatted calf? The rest of you gather lots of firewood, and we'll build a big barbecue pit."

After they'd slid back onto the ground, they rushed to do what Delphine wanted. Corgan was starved!

Beef! Real beef! Corgan stuffed himself with it. Beef and shellfish and pineapple and mango, stacked up in trays. When he couldn't hold any more, he leaned back to ask Delphine, "So how much do you know about what happened after I left Nuku Hiva last February?"

"Well," she answered, "after you left with Brigand, the Harrier jet made two more trips from the Wyo-DC to deliver supplies. And to deliver Royal—he arrived on the second trip. After that we never saw the Harrier again."

"That's because Corgan and I escaped in it when Brigand started the revolt in Wyoming," Cyborg reported. "Since we didn't know anywhere else to go, we flew to Florida."

"And I'm so, so glad you did!" Ananda said, clutching Cyborg's real hand. "Because, Delphine, Cyborg and I are . . . well, we're soul mates."

Delphine smiled indulgently. "How old did you say you are?"

"I'm fifteen," Ananda told her, "and Cyborg's sixteen, but he'll never grow any older because he's been Lockered." At the mention of the Locker, Ananda looked down at her plate, avoiding Corgan's eyes.

"I'm fifteen too," Royal said.

"Really? You look older," Sharla exclaimed. "I'd have figured you were about eighteen."

Since Sharla seemed a little too impressed by Royal, Corgan moved—casually, he hoped—to sit between them. Later, at Delphine's suggestion, they began to clear the plates from the table, a table that Royal had built, Delphine proudly told them.

"What do we do with the scraps?" Corgan asked.

"I wish we had some dogs around here to feed them to," Delphine said innocently, unaware of Ananda's stricken look. "There are a few feral cats on this island, but I don't like to encourage them because they go after baby birds." As she stacked the plates, she chattered on. "Did you kids know that dogs are descended from wolves? Genetics studies have proved that. I did my undergraduate work on dog genetics. That was a few years after they'd first been cloned successfully."

Trying to head her off from the topic, Corgan said, "That mango juice you gave us was really good, Delphine."

"Thanks." She smiled at him. "Royal made it. But what I was saying—maybe fifteen thousand years ago the wild wolves that hung around to pick up the cavemen's scraps were the ones that became domesticated. When those wolves had pups, the cavemen took care of the pups and fed them, and that's how dogs and humans bonded. We used to say, 'A man's best friend is his dog.'"

In a halting voice Ananda asked, "Then . . . there aren't any dogs here on Nuku Hiva?"

"None that I've ever seen. None that Royal's ever seen. How about you, Corgan and Cyborg? Did you see any evidence of dogs when you lived here on our island?"

Both of them shook their heads. Corgan wished Delphine would stop talking about dogs. It was Royal who seemed to clue in to Ananda's unhappiness, because he jumped up and said, "Let's take all this leftover firewood and build a big fire on the beach."

"Great idea!" Cyborg exclaimed. "Hey, Royal, want me to show you how much weight my artificial hand can carry? A lot more than you can, I bet."

"You think so? What is this—a challenge?"

"If you want it to be."

Royal would lose, Corgan knew. After Corgan and Cyborg were rescued from the toxic Atlantic, Thebos had completely disassembled Cyborg's titanium hand and put it back together twice as strong, three times as magnetic, and ten times easier to operate. "Mind if I borrow this metal tray?" Cyborg asked Delphine. Without waiting for an answer, he magnetized and stabilized the tray into perfect balance on his outstretched artificial hand. Royal was fast, but he had to pile the wood crookedly into one arm while grabbing other pieces. Cyborg had a steady platform that let him pile his stack higher and higher. Ananda, of course, was cheering for Cyborg, while Sharla rooted for Royal.

After they had built the fire, feeding it driftwood a stick at a time, it shot sparks into the darkening sky. The sky answered, one star at a time. Corgan moved away from the heat and then moved even farther away from the others to lie on his back, staring at the constellation he recognized most easily—Orion. Inside the domed cities the skies never looked this pure and clear.

"Hello, old buddy Orion," he murmured softly. "I remember the first time I saw you, back in the Wyo-DC, when I rode in the hover car with Sharla and Brig. But here you look a lot better."

From the shadows a voice said, "So do you, Corgan. You look a lot better than you did back then."

Sharla. She came toward him and dropped next to him in the sand. "I remember thinking you were too skinny then, and you had those big, strong, powerful hands that didn't seem to match the rest of your arms. But now everything about you sort of fits together. I wonder how much bigger and taller you're going to get. As big as Royal?"

"I guess I'll grow for a couple more years," he answered. "But you'll stay just the way you are for the rest of your life. Sixteen. Do you feel good about that?"

When Sharla waved her hand in the darkness, Corgan could barely see the motion. "Can we not talk about that right now?" she asked. "This is our first night on Nuku Hiva."

"Yeah. Nuku Hiva." A beat later he murmured, "Where I was happy, and you were too, weren't you? Sharla, let me ask you something." He hesitated, leaning toward her, then said, "If you had to choose between me and Brigand right now, which one would you choose?"

He could sense the indignation rising in her like heat from the sand. "Choose for what?" she flared. "To dance with? To fight a battle with? To save one of you if you both were drowning? That's a totally stupid question, and I won't even try to answer it."

She was right; it really *was* stupid! Why had he asked it—why had he spoiled the mood? Here they were, their first night on the island, when they should be trying to discover if they could ever fit together again, and he'd messed up. "I apologize," he told her. "Could we maybe take a step back and just talk about Nuku Hiva?"

"Fine with me." But she still sounded huffy and her posture was stiff. Then slowly, as a few more waves washed toward them and receded, she began to relax—Corgan knew Sharla well enough that he could tell the shifts in her moods even when she was silent. She moved closer, scooping a handful of sand and pouring it slowly onto his bare feet as she said, "I like being back here. I love listening to the waves. I really missed the ocean after we left here."

"Yes. Me too."

"Delphine seems so happy to have us here. She's gained weight since the last time I saw her, and I think I know why—there are no more flights here, so since she can't get lab supplies to work with, she cooks instead. There's plenty of food on the island," Sharla added. "Fruit, fish, fresh milk . . . all of it healthy."

"Uh-huh. Healthy." Corgan closed his eyes, picturing the delicious feast Delphine had made that evening. Slowly the picture faded, and his eyes stayed closed as Sharla went on, "It's funny, but I almost forgot how pretty it is here on Nuku Hiva. Tonight I saw one of those frigate birds, just before sunset. They look so prehistoric." She continued talking . . . and talking . . . about the moon's reflection, splintered into bright shards by the ocean waves, about how Royal seemed older than he really was, and other things . . . flowers? No, it probably wasn't flowers she'd mentioned, it was something else maybe, but Corgan hadn't caught it. He only answered "Uh-huh" every now and then as Sharla's voice grew fainter and fainter, until . . .

"You're asleep," she said.

"No, no, I'm awake, you were saying . . . uh . . . about . . ."

Brushing his lips lightly with her fingers, she told him, "It's fine. You had to stay awake way too long when you were flying us here."

Fifty-one hours and . . . he couldn't remember the minutes or seconds.

"You need the sleep," she told him. "I'll see you in the
morning."

Sleep. It felt so good. For the first time in more than four
months he could actually breathe pure, clean night air, not the
artificially controlled air inside a domed city. His mind drifted
at first into dreams of skimming over the ocean, then he fell
into a sleep so deep that he was aware of nothing—not the
gritty sand beneath him or the heat of the night, neither the
sound of the waves nor the calls of the night birds.

He had no idea how much time had passed when he felt a
nudge against his ribs. Still deep in slumber, he tried to brush
it away, but it came again, sharper this time. His eyelids raised
slowly, then flew open in horror as he saw a dark shape looming above him, bending close. Brigand! How could Brigand be
here? But he was, and he hung over Corgan, laughing cruelly,
the knife in his hand ready to stab Corgan through the heart!

Corgan rolled over and scrambled like a crab across the
sand until his hand touched a piece of driftwood. Clutching
the wood, he leaped to his feet and swung it in an arc at Brig-
and's head. *Go for the eyes!* Corgan's instincts shrieked. *Take out
his face!* The words rang inside his brain until actual shouts
penetrated his ears. "Corgan, stop! What's wrong with you?
It's me! Cyborg."

Panting, crouched forward, the wood still in his hand,
Corgan stared at Cyborg, who'd backed off, with his arms still
raised to protect his face. Bright moonlight reflected on the
metal of his artificial hand—a gleam Corgan had mistaken for
a knife. "I thought you were Brigand," he gasped.

"Well, yeah, we're clone-twins, so we look alike, but I'm the one here on the island, right? You must have had a nightmare."

The adrenaline rush caused by panic cleared Corgan's head, yet he could still feel his heart battering his rib cage. Cyborg said, "I'm sorry I scared you. Delphine sent me to tell you that Royal and you and me are supposed to sleep in the barn. She thought you wouldn't want to be out here on the sand all night."

That was right. He didn't want to stay there. The night that had seemed so peaceful not so long ago now felt full of menace, with danger lurking in the shadows of the palm fronds. Still breathing hard, he asked, "What about Sharla? Where's she sleeping?"

"First . . . put down that hunk of wood, will you? Were you really gonna hit me with that?" As Corgan let the driftwood slip slowly out of his fingers onto the sand, Cyborg said, "That's better. The girls will sleep in the laboratory with Delphine. So are you all right? Do you want to walk up to the barn with me?"

Corgan shook his head. "Go without me. I'll come up in a minute." He sank back onto the sand with his head in his hands, trying to squeeze the last threads of the dream out of his brain. The nightmare! About Brigand, his enemy.

Three

When Corgan reached the barn, Royal was already lying in one bunk, and Cyborg had just crawled into the other one. "This brings back memories," Cyborg said.

"Good or bad?" Royal asked.

"Bad. The last time I slept in this bunk, I was an eight-year-old with only one hand and a bleeding stump on the other arm."

"Yeah?" Royal raised up on an elbow. "How did that happen?"

"Later." Cyborg rolled up his LiteSuit and put it under his head for a pillow, but Royal was still curious.

"Do you take off that artificial hand when you go to bed at night?" he asked.

"Don't have to. It's comfortable and I'm used to it. Hey, Corgan, since you're the last man here, you don't get a bunk, but I piled some straw over in the corner and put a blanket on top of it. The blanket's there so if there's any creepy kind of wildlife in the straw, they won't crawl up and eat you." Cyborg and Royal both laughed like that was funny.

"Thanks. If anything tries to eat me, I'll send it your way, okay?"

"*Manuia le po,*" Royal said.

What kind of answer was that? "Huh?" Corgan grunted.

"It means 'good night.' In Samoan."

Lying on a blanket on top of straw was more comfortable than lying on sand, but after his scare on the beach Corgan had trouble getting back to sleep. Brigand's image had been so real, so threatening, looming over him in the dark! A whole hour passed before Corgan's fears disappeared along with everything else in his restless mind.

In the depths of his sleep he felt nothing until sun blazed through the barn door. Its rays baked his head, making sweat creep up into his hair. "Ooh! Hot!" he exclaimed, looking around.

He was alone. Both Royal and Cyborg had gone. Corgan stretched his arms, checking them for bug bites, then examined his chest. There were no signs of stings, but he frowned at his chest's paleness. He needed to get tan, and Nuku Hiva was the right place for it. On a hunch he crossed to the shelf where Royal's possessions lay—a razor, two shirts, a pair of shorts, and a comb. And there at the edge of the shelf, neatly folded and clean, sat Corgan's old jeans.

"Yes!" he hissed as he climbed into them. They still fit just fine, although they were a bit shorter than the last time he'd worn them.

In the other corner a few square meters of LiteCloth blocked off a small portion of the room. Corgan wondered whether Royal's curiosity had taken him in there, although he wouldn't have seen anything. Corgan pushed through the cloth, stood in front of another square of the same material, and said, "Mendor, turn on." He had to wait for only a fraction of a second before the luminous LiteCloth filled with an image.

"Corgan! How long has it been?" The shimmering pale green of the face in front of him changed to golden and then grew rosy with welcome.

"Four months, eight days, thirteen hours, nine minutes, and three and seventeen-hundredths seconds," he answered.

"Well! I see you've been keeping up your time skills." Now the face grew rounder and younger, a sign of approval.

"Yes, Mendor, I don't even try. It's just there, inside me. Did you miss me?"

"Corgan, I'm a computer program. You turned me off the day you left Nuku Hiva, and I ceased to exist until now, when you restored me." Computer program or not, Mendor looked delighted to see Corgan again.

"Mendor, a whole lot has happened, but I don't want to give you a quick rundown just yet. I want to wait till I can really fill you in, 'cause I have a lot of questions to ask you. But—"

"Just tell me how you got here, Corgan. When you closed me down, you told me you'd be leaving in the Harrier jet with Brigand and Pilot. Did they return with you?"

"No, I came back in a zero-gravity control spaceship. Without Brigand." Just saying that name made Corgan's voice drop several tones lower from pure loathing.

"Zero-gravity control?" Mendor's face slid toward the father figure image, a darker gold, verging on bronze. "How does that work, Corgan? I'd really like to know."

"It's about controlled interactions between atoms and the zero-point field. It was Thebos who figured it all out. Look, the design specifications are in the spacecraft. I'll go there later today and copy them onto a portable beam scanner so you can store the specs in your database, then I'll give the scanner to Delphine, because she's interested too. But for now I want to get your opinion on something."

"Please proceed."

Corgan hesitated. "You know how Brigand and Cyborg have this psychic connection? I mean, I know you know that, because you saw both of them together when they were little. But do you think Brigand could send his whole spirit, or phantom, or whatever, all the way through Cyborg so it would come out of him and I could see it?"

"You mean like a ghostly transmogrification?"

"Yes, I guess so. Whatever that means."

"I am a program, Corgan, and I therefore cannot confirm the presence of something as ethereal as ghosts. Projected images, yes, but that requires certain digital equipment—"

"All right, forget that question, Mendor." Corgan squirmed on the child-size stool, the one he'd built for Cyborg when he was a tiny kid, before he'd grown at that dizzying rate of two years every month. "Here's another question that's sort of on the same idea: Is it possible for an electrical process—it's called Lockering—to pass through Cyborg's brain into Brigand's when they're thousands of kilometers apart?"

"Explain Lockering."

"It's a procedure that reverses time in a person. They can go back and be younger, but then they stay that age forever. We used it on Cyborg to stop his rapid aging—and not only for that reason, but to take him back to before he got hurt in the Harrier crash . . . excuse me, Mendor, but I'd rather not explain the details right now. Too much has happened since the last time we talked, and it's hot here in the barn and I want to get into the ocean." Corgan leaned forward on the little stool. "Just tell me this, Mendor. If Lockering stopped Cyborg from premature aging, could it have gone through him and stopped Brigand's rapid aging too?"

Mendor's color changed to gray as his face altered its shape: narrower cheeks, larger forehead. "It would be easy enough to find out."

"How?"

"Just wait a little while, approach Brigand, and take a look at him. If he looks several years older than Cyborg, then it didn't happen."

"Oh, great, thanks a lot!" Corgan stood up so quickly he almost knocked over the stool. "I could have figured out that much for myself."

"Then, why didn't you?"

"Because Brigand isn't *here*. He's back in the Flor-DC, leading a revolt! Good-bye, Mendor. I'll see you later." Sometimes Mendor was no help at all.

As Corgan hustled down the hill, not quite running but going faster than walking, he took deep breaths of the humid air and rubbed his sweaty chest with his fists. He couldn't wait to get into the surf and feel those waves against his skin. Delphine would probably want him to eat something first if she saw him anywhere near the lab. What was it with grown women? It had been like that with Jane Driscoll on the space station too—when things got tense, she'd ask, "Is anyone hungry?"

To avoid Delphine, he skirted through the thick growth of trees, grabbing two bananas, which he gulped before he headed for his favorite daytime spot along the shore. When he got close, he heard shouts and laughter, and as he broke through the growth, Cyborg yelled, "Well, look who's here. It's lazy boy. You finally got up."

Ananda and Sharla still had on their LiteSuits. Soaked, the material clung to them. Cyborg was wearing some bizarre kind of greenery hat with fronds that stuck out farther than his shoulders.

"You look like a palm tree," Corgan told him.

"Don't laugh, man. Royal informed me that the art of palm weaving originated in Polynesia over five hundred years ago."

"You mean Royal made that crazy-looking hat thing for you?" Corgan questioned.

"Yes he did, man. To keep my delicate white skin from turning red as a lobster."

Redheads like Cyborg tended to fry in the sun, something Corgan had learned the hard way when he'd tended the very young Cyborg on Nuku Hiva. He'd had to stay up nights putting cool cloths on Cyborg's skin and trying to stop his howling.

"The hat isn't working," Ananda giggled. "He's already burned." She was right; Cyborg looked like he'd been scalded in a boiling pot.

"How long have you guys been out here?" Corgan asked.

"We got up to watch the sunrise," Sharla answered.

"All of you? Where was Delphine?"

"Asleep, just like you were, Corgan. Royal came with us, but then he went up to let the cattle out of the pen."

Waving toward the surf, Cyborg told him, "Come on and get your toes wet. It feels great."

"In a minute." A sense of unease washed over Corgan again—not as bad as the dread from last night, but a tightening in his chest. Cyborg had just waved, not with his good arm, but with the other. The bare, naked stump.

"Where's your artificial hand?" Corgan demanded.

"I took it off. I didn't want to get salt water on it. Salt corrodes."

The sunburn on Cyborg's right arm stretched all the way to where the wrist would have been. But then it stopped. The skin that covered the end of the stump was still pale, almost white—and dead looking. Corgan turned his eyes away to block that image.

Then Cyborg, laughing, waved his good arm and fluttered his fingers, saying, "But on the other hand . . ."

Sharla and Ananda laughed too, but Corgan muttered, "That's not funny."

"Yes it is. That was a joke, Corgan," Cyborg told him. "Lighten up."

"Yeah, come on, Corgan." Sharla ran to him and grabbed his elbow, dragging him into the waves. "I want to show you a sea turtle I saw a little while ago, if it's still out there. I made Royal promise not to spear it for turtle soup."

"You mean Royal cooks, too?"

"He says Delphine's teaching him." She dived underwater and grabbed Corgan around the knees, toppling him into the surf and then swimming away before he could catch her. Corgan gave chase. When they reached still water, both of them plunged deep, reaching for each other and holding tight as they circled and spun, until they had to rise for air, with Sharla still in his arms, their faces close together. Corgan felt his pulse quicken.

"In the *Prometheus*," she began, "I said that you made a good choice coming here. It's even better than I thought. I forgot how wonderful this place is."

"So did I." As the waves rocked them gently, Sharla didn't try to pull away.

"Even Ananda's mellowing out," she told him. "It figures. Since she spent her whole life underneath a dome, this feels like heaven to her. She said she could never swim in the Atlantic because of the pollution."

Shuddering, Corgan remembered. Horrible mutations had come at him in that ocean, wanting him for dinner. Just like Royal wanted the turtle for dinner.

After they'd drifted to a place where they could stand, Sharla rubbed the palms of her hands across his shoulders. "They're starting to turn pink," she said. "We need Royal to weave you a palm-frond hat like Cyborg's."

"There's no way I'd ever wear a freaky thing like that."

"No, I don't think you ever would. Not even to be silly, not even for fun. You're so serious, Corgan. Too serious. Have you ever acted silly?" When he frowned, trying to remember, she said, "Don't bother. I can answer that. No, you've never done anything just to be silly."

"Besides, I don't burn, I tan."

Sharla just looked at him, shaking her head. Then she shook it harder and swung her wet hair smack against Corgan's cheek.

"You'll pay for that," he sputtered, plunging after her.

Escape was not possible. He caught her by the ankles and pulled her beneath the surface, holding her underwater for a brief kiss.

When they lurched up into the air, she gasped, "Well, *that* was serious. But you didn't ask permission."

"If I'd asked, would you have let me?"

"NNTK, Corgan."

He stiffened. He hated it when she said "NNTK"—it stood for "no need to know." Usually Sharla used the term to hide something from him, like the possibility that she'd cheated to win the Virtual War. "Your shoulders are turning red," he muttered, downcast. "We better go back."

"Back to the beach, yes. But back to the way we used to be . . . just take it slower, Corgan. I don't know if it can happen."

Corgan didn't follow her out of the water.

Four

Two days later Corgan, Sharla, Cyborg, and Ananda gathered around the table to watch Royal scoop oil from a big bowl into a smaller one. "Nothing magic about it," Royal was saying. "After Cyborg got so sun-boiled, I broke open four coconuts and put the coconut milk into this bowl. I let it sit for thirty-six hours so the oil would rise to the top. It's an old Polynesian trick."

"Polynesian or Samoan? Which one are you?" Corgan asked.

"Both. Samoans are Polynesians like Frenchmen are Europeans. Or used to be, before the devastation. Okay now, Ananda, stick your fingers in here and rub the oil on Cyborg's blisters."

"Ow, ow, ow," Cyborg moaned, sounding like he had when he was a sunburned six-year-old. "But it feels better."

"From now on put it on you before you go out in the sun," Royal instructed him. "You too, Sharla. Ananda, you probably don't need it."

She nodded. "It's my Indian-Indian ancestry. But your skin's even darker than mine, Royal, so why should Polynesians—or Samoans—need the oil?"

Skimming the last drops from the top of the liquid, he answered, "You're right, it's not for sunburn. Samoan men coat themselves with oil because it makes their muscles look bigger. Watch." Royal dipped his whole hand into the coconut oil and began to rub it over his shoulders, arms, and chest. When he'd finished, he puffed out his chest and struck a pose, standing sideways, his left fist raised, his right fist on his hip.

"Oh, wow! It really works," Ananda exclaimed. "Look at those biceps!"

"Impressive." Sharla nodded, her eyes wide. "Very impressive!"

Clearing his throat, Cyborg said, "Ananda, come with me, okay? I need to talk to you about something important. Like, right away." He took her hand and pulled her toward the trees.

"That reminds me," Corgan said. "There was something I wanted to show Sharla down by the shore. 'Scuse us, Royal." Corgan would have grabbed Sharla's hand, but she pulled away.

"What are all these somethings that are suddenly so important to you and Cyborg?" she demanded as she followed Corgan, but she glanced back toward Royal, who stood alone at the table, grinning a little as he poured the coconut oil into a bottle. "I wanted to stay and get some of that sun lotion."

"You can get it later. From Delphine."

The breeze was balmy, the clouds white, the ocean gentle as Corgan motioned Sharla to come sit beside him on a fallen log at the high end of the beach. There really was something he wanted to ask her, although it wasn't especially urgent.

"So, I'm here. What?" she prompted him.

How to say it? How to talk about his anxieties when this

whole island looked like it had been created as a cradle of happiness? "Do you ever get a feeling of . . ." He hesitated. "Of . . . I don't know, like this place is haunted or something?"

"What?"

"You know. Ghosts or—"

"You brought me down here to ask me *that*? You've got to be joking." Indignant, she looked ready to get up and leave.

He backtracked quickly. "All right, all right, the truth is, I didn't like the way you were looking at Royal." At least that much was true, and it made her smile. Nothing like a little male jealousy to feed a girl's self-esteem, not that Sharla's needed much feeding.

"Well, you're being truthful about it, and that's nice. Not to worry, Corgan. Royal's cute, but Delphine's got him locked up."

Now it was Corgan's turn to be unbelieving. "Delphine? She's . . . she's old!"

"Not quite fifty. But I didn't mean she thinks of him as a boyfriend—no, nothing like that. Delphine's not creepy-weird or anything. I mean she feels like she's his mother."

"I don't know where you get these ideas, Sharla."

"Female intuition. Men just don't clue in to relationships."

They were interrupted by the sound of footsteps and Ananda calling out, "There you are. We've been trying to find you."

"Find who?" Corgan asked. "Sharla or me or both of us?"

"You, Corgan," Cyborg said. "Ananda wants to talk to you."

"She does?"

"Yeah. Privately."

"So I'll leave," Sharla said, standing up, looking a little puzzled. "Come on, Cyborg, I guess we're getting booted out."

As the two of them moved off, Ananda didn't sit down next to Corgan. She stood in front of him, seeming uncomfortable. It was the first time she and Corgan had been alone since . . . since the Flor-DC. He waited while she glanced at him, glanced away, glanced down at her fingernails, and finally said, "I'm supposed to apologize."

That was unexpected. "Why? Because Cyborg told you to?"

"Yes. And he was right." Getting those words out seemed to relax her a bit, and she sank cross-legged onto the sand in front of him. "I know I've tried to explain it to you before, Corgan, that when you grow up lonely, a dog can fill a big space in your heart. I'm not going to talk about that again, but . . . Cyborg had an idea."

"I'm listening," Corgan told her.

She dug her fingers into the sand as she said, "He was telling me how you used to work in the lab with Delphine and Grimber at night, after the cows were taken care of. And that you did this really meticulous work, something about separating zygotes implanted with genetic something or other. . . ."

"Right. Transgenic implantation. I didn't really understand the science, I just did what Delphine and Grimber told me to do, because they needed my time-splitting ability." *Where is this leading?* he wondered.

"Well, Cyborg's idea is . . . Delphine still has some of the lab equipment, even though she doesn't do any of that transgenic stuff anymore. Then the other night she told us she completed her undergraduate work in *dog genetics*! And Sharla has already done cloning—she cloned Cyborg and Brigand from Brig's cells. So . . ."

"So?" Corgan repeated.

"So we have some of Demi's cells in that food dish she used in the *Prometheus*. Cyborg thinks they'll still be viable. What if we try to clone Demi?"

Corgan was a little taken aback, but as he thought about it, the idea didn't sound too unreasonable. He scrambled the various elements in his head, letting possibilities merge and then emerge into probabilities. And while he was thinking, Ananda murmured, "Cyborg says maybe that would help settle the hard feelings between you and me." Corgan was about to answer that most of the hard feelings were on Ananda's side, but she added, "He says we'll have to ask the experts, Delphine and Sharla, if it can be done."

Cyborg, Cyborg—was any of this Ananda's plan? But she was the one who'd actually come to him, so Corgan agreed, "Okay, let's go." He jumped up and started off for the lab, then halted to wait for Ananda, remembering that he was supposed to be more . . . what was it Cyborg always accused him of *not* being? Sensitive! Aware of other people's feelings. "We can walk up there together," he told Ananda.

Apparently Cyborg hadn't mentioned any of this to Sharla, because she was not in the lab when they arrived. Corgan stopped just inside the door, surprised at how different the place looked now. Flowers radiated their tropical colors everywhere, their stalks thrust into laboratory beakers because Delphine had no vases.

"We came to talk to you about something, Delphine," Ananda announced hesitantly.

"Well, come right in. I welcome the company. Have a seat." Delphine arranged herself on her own chair, pulling her skirt over her knees.

"That dress is really pretty," Ananda began.

"I made it myself, out of tapa cloth. I made the tapa cloth too, out of breadfruit bark. If you like, I can show you how to do that, but I suspect that isn't the reason for this visit."

"No, it isn't," Corgan answered. Ananda found a chair while Corgan sat down on a rough-hewn bench, which was probably another of Royal's handcrafts. "We were wondering if it's possible for you and Sharla to make a clone of Demi," he announced. "There might be some viable cells in a bowl she ate from."

Delphine had been wrapping a headband around her thick, wild hair, but she stopped suddenly. The abundant hair swirled as she shook her head no. "Can't be done. Here's the problem, kids. I'll try to keep it simple so you can understand. When you worked here with the cattle, Corgan, we implanted genetically altered cows' eggs—where? Into other cattle. Where they would gestate. And when Sharla created the two clones from Brig's cells, she gestated one in an artificial womb and the other inside a mutant girl, a human. Well, I don't have an artificial womb here in the laboratory . . ."

"Couldn't you just put the cloned cells into one of the cows?" Ananda asked, still hopeful.

"Won't work. Implanting into different species is next to impossible. I need a dog. A female dog. And we don't have any of those here on the island."

Corgan frowned, trying to come up with a solution. One seemed fairly obvious. "Would a cat work? There are a couple of feral cats here on Nuku Hiva, and I could trap them."

"Nope. I just told you—I'd need a female dog. Let me explain a little. The basic method involves placing an adult animal's DNA, extracted from, say, a skin cell, which you said you have, into an egg cell *from the same species* after the egg cell has had its DNA removed. It's then implanted into a surrogate mother, *again of the same species*. Cows to cows, sheep to sheep, dogs to dogs."

In the silence Corgan could hear water dripping, one drop at a time, from Delphine's distillation unit. "What if I could find a dog?" he suggested, thinking out loud. "The Isles of Hiva are a chain of islands, Mendor told me—ten islands. Only one other one's as big as Nuku Hiva. I'm thinking that since wild boars and feral cats have managed to survive here on Nuku Hiva, other animals may have survived on other islands in the chain, especially the bigger one, Hiva Oa. Maybe there are feral dogs there. I could go and look for them."

Ananda brightened, but Delphine appeared skeptical, asking, "You mean, fly the *Prometheus* from here to Hiva Oa, and if there are no dogs there, then fly to all the smaller islands?"

Corgan shook his head. "I wouldn't want to use up fuel in a wild-goose chase—or a wild-dog chase. I need to keep enough fuel to . . ." To keep his options open. "I'm thinking of another way," he told Delphine. "I could build a boat."

"A boat! You don't have the slightest idea how to build a boat," Delphine objected.

"Mendor could help me. And so could Royal."

"And so could I!" Ananda chimed in. "I don't know

whether Corgan has told you, but I've been genetically enhanced to be the strongest female on the planet."

"Think sensibly!" Delphine cried. "Neither you nor Corgan nor Royal would have the slightest idea how to build a boat. Even if you did make one, you'd get out in the waves and capsize and drown."

Corgan leaned forward on the bench, his hands on his knees. "Hey, Delphine, I'm not trying to be disrespectful, because you're a good person and I like you a lot," he told her. "But you're not our mother. You act like a mother and that's nice, in a way, because we don't have any actual mothers. But Delphine, you can't tell us what to do. We're in—"

"—dependent," Ananda finished. "Independent means we don't have to take orders, Delphine. I don't think it's such a terrible idea to build a boat and go looking for wild dogs."

"That's completely crazy." Delphine's eyes began to widen in alarm. "You're just kids!"

"We're not 'just kids,'" Ananda answered softly. "None of us is ordinary. We're all products of laboratory manipulation, all except Royal, I guess, and I don't know much about him except he seems pretty strong too."

"We're not talking about speed and strength here," Delphine argued. "We're talking about engineering ability and carpentry skills and experience and decent judgment, which none of you is old enough to have. You're just kids!"

"You already said that," Ananda answered. "Maybe one of the things you forgot to mention is courage. Corgan and I have that; I don't know about Royal."

Delphine jumped up. "I don't want you taking Royal on such a foolhardy venture!"

What Sharla had said seemed right on target—Delphine felt like Royal's mother. Keeping himself out of the discussion, Corgan began to think about boats. During his earlier stay on Nuku Hiva he'd explored every section of the island and every meter of its coastline, and there were no boats rotting in the sun or decomposing on the shore. Not even pieces of one. They'd have to make one from scratch. Corgan felt sure Mendor would have the necessary instructions somewhere in his/her computer data storage system.

They'd need wood and nails. Royal had built the table where they dined outside under the palms, so maybe he had enough leftover nails for a boat. Trees were plentiful; they could be cut down and sliced. All this was going to take time.

He thought about manpower—or womanpower. Cyborg had been injured because of the crash into the Atlantic, but he was fine now that he'd been Lockered; he could help with the work. Corgan couldn't picture Sharla with a hammer in her hand, but maybe she'd surprise him. And Delphine—if she realized they were serious about this, she'd have to quit arguing against it. Or maybe not.

"Okay," he said as he stood up to leave the lab. "I'm going to run this through Mendor's database to get some information."

As he hurried from the lab, Ananda and Delphine were still arguing, Delphine's voice rising in opposition as Ananda's lowered obstinately. He was so caught up in the possibilities that he hardly noticed where he was going until he nearly ran into Sharla. Kneeling a dozen meters away inside the shelter of the trees, she was pounding something with a rock.

"You look like you're killing it, whatever it is," he called to her. "What are you doing?"

"Making a dress like Delphine's."

"By beating it to death?"

"Sort of."

For a moment Corgan forgot that he was on his way to quiz Mendor, because finding Sharla alone was a luxury. She didn't have to explain why she was pounding; Corgan recognized the process of making tapa cloth out of the bark of the breadfruit tree. He'd watched Delphine do it when he lived on the island earlier. Dropping to his knees beside Sharla, he asked, "Need some help?"

"Sure. You can thump it for a while 'cause my arm's getting tired. I'll strip some more bark from the branches."

"Why are you doing this?" he asked as he lifted the mango-size rock from her hand. "It takes a long time to turn this stuff into cloth—you have to strip it, pound it, soak it, paste it, dry it out—"

She interrupted, "Because I don't have anything to wear except this one LiteSuit, which really belongs to you, and it's too big for me." She ran her fingers down the front of the gold LiteSuit, making the fabric shimmer in reflected sunlight. With her hair matching the LiteSuit, she looked like a priceless gold figurine. He kept pounding, but he kept glancing sideways at her too.

After the bark had softened enough, he rose to his feet and said, "Gotta go."

"Where?"

"To consult with Mendor."

"You're leaving me for Mendor?" She laughed a little as she said it.

"After I talk to Mendor, I'll be back to explain everything to you. But . . ." He paused, enjoying his dramatic moment. "In a couple of days I might be out of here."

He left her kneeling in front of the tapa cloth, looking surprised.

Five

"First," Mendor the father figure told Corgan, "you must find a tree with a trunk about thirty meters high and at least one meter thick. Then you cut it down and—"

"Thirty meters high! How am I supposed to cut down a tree that big?" Corgan demanded.

"That will be for you to decide, Corgan," Mendor answered, his eyes gleaming harshly in his dark gray digital image. "My computer database has instructions for a Polynesian dugout canoe that holds one hundred warriors, the kind that once crossed the Pacific Ocean. Unfortunately, I have no instructions for anything smaller than that."

"This is the second useless answer I've had from you since I came back," Corgan complained. "What's with you, Mendor?"

Never before had he seen Mendor's face slide so rapidly from father to mother. Bright pink, Mendor cried, "You go away and leave me for four months, and then you come back here and I'm supposed to be as good as I was before!"

"Huh!" Corgan was dumbfounded.

"Sorry." The features slid again, still female, but darker. "Sorry, sorry. That outburst sounded like emotion, didn't it, and computer programs are not supposed to have emotions."

Was that a tear on Mendor's cheek? Something was definitely wrong. Corgan pulled aside the sheet that the Mendor images reflected from and stared down at the operations box behind it. The box lay open on the floor, spread wide, but that wasn't the problem—the operations box was versatile enough that it could be compacted to the dimensions of a deck of cards or expanded to suitcase size.

The real problem was obvious. A narrow beam of sunlight shone down from the roof onto the ramification gear inside the box. Corgan fingered the gear and found it hot to the touch.

"Ouch!" he heard Mendor say. "Please stop. That really hurts."

"Okay, I see what's wrong," he called to Mendor. "Some of the thatch must have blown off the roof, and it's letting hot sun hit your fibril connectors. I'll go fix it right now."

Climbing with hands and knees, he worked his way up the post that supported the roof, wondering as he scaled it who had actually built this barn. And who had built Delphine's laboratory? Both buildings had been in place before Corgan landed on the island right after the Virtual War. When he reached the roof, he crawled to the spot above Mendor's box, and as he'd guessed, very little thatch remained on that section. He'd have to come back later with armloads of palm to cover the bare spots, but for now he could close up the hole that was causing the trouble.

When he began to scrape away some of the loose thatch, his hand touched metal. Cautiously he felt underneath and discovered . . . the knife!

For a long time Corgan sat holding it, staring at it. The

knife edge, when he touched it, was still sharp, and the metal was so shiny he saw his eyes reflected in it. The blade, thirty-five centimeters long and five wide, broadened where it curved upward at the point. During his first stay on Nuku Hiva he'd used the knife often to clear jungle growth.

When was the last time he'd seen it? As he leaned back, brilliant sunlight penetrated his closed eyelids and he saw red, the color of blood. And he remembered. It was the day he'd nearly killed Brigand in battle, a twelve-year-old Brigand who'd attacked Corgan with this same knife. Corgan had fought back with a spear, and as he'd stood above Brigand, the spear poised over the boy's heart, he'd hesitated. Too long. He should have killed Brigand right then and there. How many innocent lives would have been spared if Corgan had plunged that spear into the young Brigand, the future assassin, who two months afterward would execute the entire Wyoming Supreme Council? By now Brigand had killed countless others, murdering anyone who opposed him.

Corgan's memory backtracked further. Two months before that nearly fatal battle with Brigand, when the clone-twins had been only eight years old—he shuddered as the grisly recollection tormented his mind's eye: Corgan carelessly leaving the knife beside the pool; little Cyborg crashing into the pool, where a rockslide trapped him beneath a boulder; Brigand taking the knife and . . . "Stop this!" Corgan hissed to himself, trying to force the images out of his mind. He felt invaded by the memory, as if the knife held a curse.

Or maybe he was imagining things. This knife was probably nothing more than a tool left behind years ago by one of the island natives and discovered by Corgan when he first came to Nuku Hiva. He couldn't even remember where he'd found it. But he couldn't *stop* remembering what it had done to Cyborg.

After he covered the hole in the roof with nearby thatch, Corgan climbed down, taking the knife with him. Royal stood waiting for him at the door of the barn, barefoot, wearing nothing but a ragged pair of pants cut off at the knees.

"Where'd you get that?" Royal asked.

"The knife? I found it on the roof."

"On the roof? Weird! Only it's not a knife," Royal said, pointing at it as he explained, "It's a machete. There's a difference between a knife and a machete. Who does it belong to?"

"I don't know. No one, I guess." Corgan wanted to change the subject. "So what are *you* doing up here?"

Royal gave a little shrug. "I just came to find out if you'd asked Mendor how to make a canoe."

"How did you know about that?" Corgan wondered. Not much more than half an hour had passed since the scene in the lab, and when Corgan left there, Ananda and Delphine had still been arguing.

"There's only six of us on this island, Corgan," Royal answered. "It's pretty hard to keep anything secret. So what did your . . . your . . . I don't know what to call your Mendor because I don't know what exactly it is. But it doesn't matter what Mendor said because I already know how to build a canoe."

"You do?"

"Yeah. My grandfather taught me—it's in our blood. I can make a real special canoe that three people can paddle all at the same time. You, me, and Ananda."

"What about Sharla and Cyborg? Maybe they'll want to go along."

"It'll be a three-person canoe, and we need the three strongest persons to paddle it. That's you, Ananda, and me."

Corgan said, "Yeah, Royal, if you can ever get yourself away from Delphine."

"Because of the cows? I'll just turn them out to pasture till we get back, and she can milk the ones that need milking. She doesn't mind that."

"No," Corgan answered, "because she wants to keep you here where she can watch over you."

Royal's dark brows lowered as he straightened his back and declared, "Hey, Corgan, I'm not Delphine's servant. I'm the boss of myself. I do what I want to do, and right now I want to make a dugout canoe, and that means we need a tree."

"All right!" They smacked fists and started down the hill toward the beach. Corgan glanced from side to side, checking every tree they passed until Royal told him, "Stop looking at trees that stand up. Look for ones that got blown over by cyclones."

"That'd be smarter," Corgan agreed.

"Look for a trunk we can trim to three meters long."

"Three meters long and how wide?" Corgan asked.

"Big enough to fit our butts. That's all."

Corgan took a quick check of Royal's butt, which was wider than his own but about the same size as Ananda's. "That'll work," he said. "Three butts in a boat."

Both of them laughed at that, but then, remembering Delphine's arguments, Corgan grew quiet, wondering if the dog hunt might turn out to be all for nothing. He was about to mention that when Royal announced, "Over there. That one."

The tree must have blown down some time ago because its branches were bare except for ground foliage creeping across them. A fat, scaly lizard sat on one of the branches, staring at them, insolent and unafraid. Corgan's eyes traveled from the ripped-out roots that pointed skyward to a usable section of trunk he figured could be trimmed to a length of three meters.

"Use that machete in your hand," Royal said. "We'll chop off the branches and slide the trunk down the hill, down to the beach. I have a hatchet, but it's back at the lab. I'll go get it. You wait here, Corgan."

After Royal left and the lizard skittered away, Corgan straddled the trunk of the fallen tree, picturing it as a canoe sturdy enough to sail the seas or at least the narrow passages from island to island. The trunk was about two thirds of a meter thick, wide enough to be hollowed into a thin-sided canoe. First they'd have to chop off the branches, as Royal had said. Corgan looked around and decided that moving the tree downhill wouldn't be easy because of all that thick growth they'd have to drag it through, the gnarled and twisted roots that snaked everywhere. They'd probably need to carry it on their shoulders most of the way to the beach, where they'd have room to work. He wondered how much the log would weigh after it got trimmed.

When Royal returned, Ananda and Cyborg were with him. "Royal told us what you're doing," Cyborg said. "We were trying to figure how we could help when there are only two chopping tools. Then I had this idea."

"Cyborg's so smart," Ananda said for what must have been the thousandth time in the past two months.

"Here's what I thought," Cyborg continued. "Sixty years ago or so people lived on this island, before plague wiped them out. They probably had houses with sheet-metal roofs and lots of other things made of metal. I bet some of it is still on the island, buried under the sand or covered by all this vegetation."

"So?" Corgan queried, getting up off the log.

"So if I trek around the island with the magnetism turned on in my artificial hand—I mean, turned to the highest strength—pieces of metal will get magnetized and pop up out of the sand. Or out of the leaves. We'll recover whatever's useful, just like the Hydrobots do back in the Flor-DC."

Slipping her arm through Cyborg's, Ananda added, "I'll bend the salvage into scraping tools to dig out the wood from inside the trunk. Maybe into cutting tools too."

That made a lot of sense. "We could use a fire to shape the tools," Corgan said.

"Not 'we,'" Ananda told him. "You already have the machete to work with, and Royal has a hatchet. This project is for Cyborg and me." She tightened her arm in his.

"So let's get started," Royal said.

"I'll clear away the vines," Corgan offered as he grabbed the machete—he had to remember to call it that—by the blade, feeling its sharp edge once again against his skin. Suddenly he felt a pull on his palm. Within microseconds it grew stronger and hotter, until the machete got ripped out of his fist. "Hey!" he yelled. "What happened?"

And then he knew. Cyborg had switched on his arm's

magnetic force, setting up a vibration that made the machete's metal blade leap across space and stick fast to Cyborg's magnetized titanium palm.

"Whoo! You better be careful doing that," Corgan shouted. "You could have cut me!"

"Yeah. I could have. That would have been ironic—isn't this the knife Brigand used to slice off my right hand?"

It was the scene Corgan had tried to block from his memory—little Cyborg lying nearly drowned on the bank of the pool, bleeding from his right wrist, which no longer had a hand attached to it; Brigand crying that the only way he could save Cyborg from the boulder that trapped him underwater was to cut off his hand; Corgan furious because he knew that was a lie.

"Don't look so freaked out," Cyborg was telling him now. "It was just a demonstration of how metal will react to my artificial hand." He wiggled the titanium fingers, saying, "This baby comes in handy—hey, did you get that? Handy?"

"Funny," Royal responded, not smiling.

Cyborg shrugged, then said, "Come on, Ananda, let's go." He threw the machete into the ground, point first, handle up, embedding it deeply in the dirt.

After they left, crossing at an angle through the trees, Corgan picked up the knife and held it between his forefinger and thumb. If he hadn't needed it to build a canoe, he'd have run down to the shore and heaved it into the ocean. Nuku Hiva, though beautiful, seemed to be having a strange effect not just on Corgan, but on everyone.

Reading Corgan's thoughts, Royal said, "Ghosts."

"Huh?"

"I believe in ghosts. Many people died here from plague before the devastation."

"Yeah. I saw somebody die here too," Corgan said, "but not from plague. Grimber, Delphine's partner. He had a heart attack and fell down dead right in front of me and Delphine. She wasn't even sorry 'cause Grimber was such a mean scum."

"You buried his body in the sand, right? Delphine told me," Royal answered. "Bad ghosts like that don't go away, they just go into hiding."

If there were ghosts, this brooding tropical island would be the place to find them. It was here the spirit of a cannibal chief had entered Brigand, or so he claimed, right before he cut off Cyborg's hand. Ghosts didn't seem to worry Royal, though. In this dark, damp forest where moisture dripped from the leaves onto Royal's cheeks like tears, he hummed as he hacked away at the branches. Suddenly he gave a yell in Samoan.

"What?" Corgan asked, but Royal just pointed. The hatchet had uncovered . . . bones! Two bones, one long and one broken. "Human?" Corgan asked.

Royal nodded. "Leg bone."

Corgan peered closer at the bleached bones. He noticed faint notches on one and a slice mark on the other, maybe from a knife blade. "Look at that! This guy might have been murdered," he said. "Mendor told me the people who lived here were cannibals who ate their enemies."

Royal frowned, his eyes narrowing. "That was hundreds of years ago. Anyway, don't believe everything you hear about Pacific Islanders. A lot of it is just made-up stuff." He picked up one of the bones, then threw it almost savagely into the underbrush, saying, "Those marks were made from animals chewing on them. Probably wild boars. I'm gonna go find another tree."

Had Corgan said something offensive? Were Samoans cannibals too, hundreds of years ago? Should he apologize or just shut up? He chose the latter and hurried to catch up to Royal, who was stalking down the hill.

It was going well. Corgan used the machete to shape the bow, while Royal roughed out the canoe body with the hatchet. Cyborg, Sharla, and Ananda hollowed the softer insides of the trunk using tools they'd made from the salvaged scrap metal.

"Let's move it, you guys," Corgan called out. "We haven't even started to trim the float for the outrigger, and then Royal has to show us how to attach it."

Royal kept chipping wood to shape the stern, again humming a tune under his breath as he worked. "What's that song, Royal?" Sharla asked. "Sing it for us."

"Ah, you don't want to hear that."

"Why not?"

"Because I'm a terrible singer."

"Oh, come on, Royal," Ananda joined in. "You sounded pretty good just then. Sing it out loud."

"Okay." Royal set down the hatchet, grinning as he gave a little bow, then began:

> "Fonuea, Fonuea, Laulau mai se Manamea,
> O sa ai e i luga nei? O sa Letuli e i luga nei.
> A ua ina, a la ina, O le a solo mata'iga,
> Laulau tu la le i'a, Ususu!"

"What does it mean?" Sharla asked.

"Mmmm . . . it means, if I get it right . . ." Royal waved his fingers as though trying to pluck the words and music out of the air. "It means, 'Bring to me this lovely pair / Who are they that linger there?'"

"Uh-*huh*! He's singing about Ananda and Sharla," Cyborg declared. "'This lovely pair.'"

Royal laughed so hard he almost doubled over. When he caught his breath, he said, "The lovely pair are a turtle and a shark. So which one of these girls is a turtle and which is a shark? Ananda, who are you?"

"I'll be the shark," she answered. "I'll take a bite out of your neck and spit you into the ocean."

"That means Sharla is a turtle," Corgan yelled.

"Oh, great! So I'm slow and toothless." As Corgan started to run, Sharla threw a seashell at him that hit him square in the back. He yelled, but it hadn't hurt. They'd been working so hard they needed a break. It was fun to play for a while, tossing a coconut back and forth as in a game of Go-Ball, kicking up sand as they ran, hooting when Cyborg dropped the toss. Fun until Delphine appeared, looking stern.

They abruptly stopped their clowning and stood still, ill at ease.

"So, you're really going ahead with this?" Delphine asked, standing before them with her feet planted firmly in the sand, her hands behind her back.

"Looks like it, Delphine," Corgan answered.

"You know that I am adamantly against this venture."

All of them nodded and murmured, "We know."

"You made it clear enough," Ananda said.

"Well, since nothing I say seems to dissuade you, I want you to know that I've been reading Grimber's logbook. He kept records of the weather. If the atmosphere is really clear, according to his journal, you may actually be able to see the different islands in the distance."

"See them? You mean real sightings?" Corgan exclaimed.

"On the clearest days, from right here on Nuku Hiva, you can see as far as eighty kilometers out to sea, Grimber wrote. That could help you—although I will continue to hope and pray that you forget this ridiculous idea, which is totally without merit." She looked from one to the other, but none of them moved or answered.

"And so," she continued, "if you are lucky, you might be able to sight a destination quickly."

"Right." They were already lucky in one way—it wasn't cyclone season, so they shouldn't be blown all the way to . . . to wherever cyclones blew canoes in this part of the Pacific.

Delphine went on, "I've made the three of you new shirts out of tapa cloth so you won't get too sunburned." She suddenly brought her arms forward and held the shirts out to them. "I didn't have time to decorate the cloth very much," she said, "but you'll notice each one has a figure on it of a little dog. I painted them with kava juice."

That Delphine—what a class act! Corgan thought. He and Royal and Ananda crowded around her, thanking her enthusiastically as they accepted the shirts and pulled them over their heads, Ananda squirming into hers even though she had to slide it over her LiteSuit. Delphine accepted their thanks graciously but with enough reserve to let them know that nothing could make her approve of this crazy venture they insisted upon.

The next day the canoe began to take shape almost before their eyes. And Royal gave it a name: *Tuli*.

The seabird.

Six

"One, two, three—launch!" Corgan yelled.

With Royal in front, Ananda in the middle, and Corgan last, they shoved the *Tuli* across sand into shallow water. *Let it float, let it float,* Corgan pleaded silently as the heavy dugout canoe slid into water, which got deeper and deeper, and then, "It floats!" all three of them shouted. They scrambled inside and grabbed the paddles. This test drive was mainly to find out if the *Tuli* would stay on top of the water and not sink like a stone.

On the shore the other three islanders stood watching— Sharla waving, Cyborg a little farther away with an expression of doubt on his sunburned face, Delphine looking scared.

"Start paddling," Royal ordered from his seat in the front.

Gripping the top of the paddle with his left hand, Corgan slid his right hand to about fifteen centimeters above the blade. The shaft felt smooth; Sharla had polished it with crushed coral. He dipped the blade into the gentle waves to the right of him and pulled back against the water's resistance. That wasn't so hard. Ahead of him Royal did the same, while Ananda, between them, paddled on the left, inside the outrigger.

"Are we trying to circle around?" Corgan asked, because the canoe was turning back toward shore.

"No! You need to paddle on the other side," Royal answered.

"The outrigger side?"

"Yeah. Behind the outrigger."

"Oh." Something wasn't working. No matter how hard Corgan pulled on the paddle, the *Tuli* made zero progress in the placid bay. He stroked from front to back but noticed Royal sometimes paddling from back to front—shouldn't they be doing the same thing? When the *Tuli* started rocking in the water, Ananda yelled, "Hey, you guys! Coordinate!"

"You steer, Royal, and I'll row," Corgan called as the canoe turned completely around, facing the shore, where Sharla held her hands over her mouth because she was laughing and pretending not to. Delphine held her own hands over her eyes, unable to watch.

"No, the guy in the back is supposed to steer," Royal yelled.

Corgan tightened his fists on the paddle. What was wrong here? He'd flown the *Prometheus*, the most advanced space-craft ever designed, flown it up above Earth's atmosphere without a single flight error. And here he was in this ancient form of transportation, used thousands of years ago by primitive aborigines, and he was floundering in the waves like an upside-down turtle. Ears burning with humiliation, he muttered, "We're gonna stay out here till we get this stupid thing to work."

"Let's change seats," Ananda said.

"No!" Corgan could just picture what would happen if they tried to change positions out there on the water—the boat would capsize, all three of them would end up in the drink, and Sharla would collapse onto the sand giggling.

"Have you ever paddled a canoe before?" Royal asked Corgan.

"No. You?"

"No."

"Both of you, turn off the testosterone and use your brains," Ananda told them. "Right now we're all working *against* one another. We have to work together. Lift your paddles out of the water while we figure this out."

Corgan wished Cyborg could be with them. Corgan and Ananda were strong and powerful, and Royal's muscles bulged even without the coconut oil, but Cyborg had the smarts they needed, the sharp intuition that keyed to the core of unfamiliar situations. After fifteen minutes of floating around, experimenting and splashing so much they were all soaked, Royal said, "Let's go back. I need to get some advice."

They managed to turn the canoe and head toward shore, where tall palms stood like sentinels guarding the lush greenery. After they had shoved the *Tuli* onto the beach, Cyborg told them, "Looks like you guys used four times as much effort to get half as far as you wanted to go. We need to figure out the mechanics of three people paddling at the same time."

"No problem," Royal panted, brushing sand from his feet. "I'm gonna ask my grandfather how to do it."

The silence that followed was broken when Sharla said cautiously, "Your *grandfather*?"

"Yeah. He's been giving me all the instructions for building the *Tuli*. I just did what he told me."

"Uh . . . when did he give you those instructions?" Corgan inquired. "A long time ago?"

"No. Every night while we were working on the *Tuli*, my grandfather would come into my dreams and tell me what to do."

The silence lasted longer this time, until Ananda stammered, "I—I can understand that, maybe. It's sort of like that psychic connection between Brigand and Cyborg. Isn't it?"

Shaking his head, Royal told them, "Not exactly. My grandfather died before I was born."

"Uh, then you never knew him," Corgan stated, trying hard to make sense out of this.

"Sure I know him. I told you, he comes to me in dreams and tells me how to do things, how to be a man. See, before the devastation, missionaries brought my family to Utah. After the nuclear blast my grandfather sealed all the family into a trailer and drove to the Wyoming domed city, because it wasn't very far from Utah to Wyoming. The family survived because they were sealed so tight in the trailer that radiation couldn't get to them, but my grandfather didn't have any protection 'cause he was driving. He died a little later of radiation poisoning. He was a great man. I want to be just like him."

Looking almost ready to faint, Delphine gasped, "And this is why you decided you could build a seaworthy canoe, because you dream of your grandfather?"

Royal looked from one to the other. "What's the problem?" he asked.

As they glanced anxiously at one another, Corgan said, "I think we need to have a meeting."

Grimly Delphine answered, "Gather around the table. I'll put out food."

The discussion heated up as everyone added fuel to their

arguments—Ananda saying that she couldn't see a lot of difference between the Brigand-Cyborg connection and Royal's visits from his grandfather; Cyborg answering that yes it was different, because he and his clone-twin were both alive and Royal's grandfather was dead. Corgan said that it didn't matter how they had gotten the instructions because the *Tuli* seemed to be seaworthy, and if Royal's grandfather could just teach them how to paddle, they ought to be able to manage just fine.

Delphine's arguments were the most vehement. She'd objected to the whole idea right from the beginning, she reminded them, and she didn't believe in visits from the dead or channeling or whatever else it was called. She was a scientist. Scientists didn't go off on harebrained adventures using questionable or inferior apparatus. Even though the dugout canoe had *appeared* to be seaworthy, they'd tested it only on placid seas, and who knew what would happen in a storm? Scientists would demand much more proof, and so should they. "You kids, your heads are just too far away from reality!" she cried.

Throughout it all Royal sat silent, looking a little hurt. Finally Sharla announced, "This is going nowhere. Only three people are involved in this expedition, and they'll have to decide for themselves. The rest of us should stay out of it."

Royal, Ananda, and Corgan exchanged looks. Finally Ananda reached out to cover Royal's hand with her own and said, "I'm in."

"Me too," Corgan declared, making it a three-person handgrip.

"So it's settled. Let's have a farewell around the fire," Sharla suggested. "All of us. You too, Delphine."

Reluctantly Delphine rose to her feet. Nodding stiffly, she said, "All of you may live to regret this. That is, I *hope* you live. There's nothing more I can say, so go ahead and get the fire started. I'll bring the mango juice."

After an hour of sitting quietly near the campfire, the six of them began to drift into pairs. Sharla and Corgan found a sheltered spot where waves crashed against a pile of rocks. Ananda and Cyborg disappeared somewhere, while Delphine and Royal stayed next to the fire, with Delphine leaning forward arguing fervently, apparently still trying to talk Royal out of making the trip. All six were aware that the next morning three of them would stay behind on Nuku Hiva while Corgan, Ananda, and Royal left the island on a mission that could end in failure. Or worse.

The moon had shrunk by nearly half, but it still cast enough light that Corgan could see Sharla in shadow. He reached out to brush her cheek with his fingertips, and as she turned toward him, his lips moved close to hers.

"Are you sure you want to do this?" she asked.

"Uh . . . kiss you?"

"Not that," she said, laughing a little and moving away. "I know you want to do that. I mean tomorrow—are you absolutely sure you want to take that clumsy dugout canoe out into the ocean just to search for a dog? It doesn't seem like a good enough reason. What if you don't come back?"

"Would you be sorry if I didn't come back?"

"You know I would. You're the only one who can pilot the *Prometheus*. If anything happened to you, I'd be stuck on this island forever. I mean, it's a nice enough island, but I want to go back to Florida. Eventually."

Go back to Brigand—that's what she really meant, Corgan thought. *That's all she ever cared about. Brigand.* If Corgan did drown in the Pacific, trapping Sharla forever on Nuku Hiva, it would serve her right. He moved away from her.

"Oh, Corgan, I'm sorry," she said as she reached out to him. "I was genetically engineered to be a code breaker, not a strategist like Cyborg, and I say dumb things sometimes. Of course I'd be sorry if you didn't come back. We have a history, you and I. And right now if you still want to kiss me, then . . . it's okay."

Did he still want to? Not as much as before, but he leaned closer to her, waiting for his feelings to tell him where to go next.

"Time to shove off," Corgan was about to shout, but then he remembered that Royal had declared himself captain. The *Tuli* had been packed with basics, as many as they could jam beneath the three rough-hewn crossways seats. At the bottom lay the machete, Royal's hatchet, and a cattle prod that arced sparks, useful for scaring wild animals and for starting fires. A cowhide container that Delphine had stitched held water, but probably not enough for three persons on a strenuous day. As for food, they had a few coconuts, bananas, and breadfruit. They figured they'd easily find food on whatever islands they reached, the same fruits and fish that were so abundant on Nuku Hiva.

"The sun's up, the wind's down, and once you get into the *Tuli*, I'll teach you how my grandfather said to paddle," Royal announced.

Sharla, Delphine, and Cyborg stood on the beach to see

them off, Delphine looking afraid that the *Tuli* might not make it past the first breakers. After the three sailors had pushed the *Tuli* into the water and climbed in, Royal cried out, "Listen good," and he began to relay instructions from his grandfather, or so he claimed. Royal should paddle on the right side. Ananda, in the middle position, would paddle on the left, inside the outrigger. It would be tricky for her to keep from hitting the bamboo rods that held the float in place— she'd have to be careful, or she could knock the outrigger apart. Seated in the stern, Corgan was supposed to steer. Royal told him that a paddle stroke that moved the bow to the left would move the stern to the right and rotate the canoe. When finally the three of them managed to stroke with the same rhythm, the *Tuli* shot ahead nice and straight, while Corgan turned quickly to wave good-bye. Royal's grand-father's lesson seemed to be working.

They were heading out to sea with no compass, no charts, nothing to let them know where they were going except the position of the rising sun. By luck, the sea looked flat and the sky was so clear they could see for a distance of about thirty kilometers. All three of them paddled in smooth rhythm, gaining far more speed than Corgan expected; in fact, they were traveling amazingly fast. *Muscle power,* Corgan thought. Two genetically designed superpeople and one Samoan prince were making the seabird fly.

"I'll be the lookout," Ananda announced. "My vision is better than normal."

"You do that." Corgan concentrated, trying to remember every detail of the map Mendor had found for him. The biggest island in the chain, other than Nuku Hiva, was called

Hiva Oa, and it lay to the southeast. That was the one they should logically visit first, since its size might mean it had more flora and fauna than the others. But they seemed to be heading due south, although Corgan couldn't be sure. He'd spent so much of his life underneath a dome that he had no experience using the sun to figure out directions.

They hadn't gone all that far when Ananda cried, "There! I see it! I see an island."

"It can't be Hiva Oa," Corgan answered. "We haven't traveled far enough. Hiva Oa's supposed to be a hundred twenty kilometers from Nuku Hiva."

"Who cares if it's Hiva Oa?" she called back. "Any island in the chain might have dogs, and at least we can see where we're going if we row to this one first."

"I agree," Royal said. "One island is as good as another."

Maybe it would be easier on their first day out to head for a landfall they could actually see, even though now it was no more than a slight gray brown swelling on the horizon. Once again he pictured Mendor's chart and then announced, "I guess that one's Ua Pou. It's pretty close, so we should be able to reach it. We can search the whole island if we get there before sunset, and then shove off for Hiva Oa tomorrow."

"Exactly how far is it to Ua Pou?" Ananda asked.

"I think Mendor told me it's about forty kilometers from Nuku Hiva, and we've already gone around five. We should get there in a few more hours if no storms blow up."

Letting his brain go numb, Corgan turned his arms into mechanical levers that pumped at a steady, unchanging beat: dip the paddle forward, pull it back, swing it forward again, repeat the motion nonstop without trying to count the strokes. Just grip it and rip it. Every now and then he'd call out to Royal or Ananda to switch sides, and they would react instantly, swinging their paddles from the right side to the left side or the other way around. Once they got the hang of it, it was amazing how much speed they picked up, skimming faster and faster over the surface of the sea. They made a powerful, synchronized team.

In spite of the boring, repetitive motion Corgan's mind wouldn't stay still. He kept reliving last night, when he'd sat next to Sharla in the darkness of the bay. How he wished he could force his fingers inside her skull to pull out every last fragment of Brigand that lurked there, poisoning her. Sure, she'd let Corgan kiss her, and she'd seemed to like it, but he knew he never had all of her, all her attention or warmth or caring or involvement. Last night Corgan had been the one who pulled away, wondering if she was comparing him with Brigand.

"I'm getting thirsty," Ananda announced. Using the machete, she split the tops off three coconuts so they could drink the juice. Then they ate bananas, one person at a time while the other two paddled. Then the breadfruit. Hours went by as the strange island—probably Ua Pou—kept growing taller and wider ahead of them, its peaks thrusting upward from the ocean like spear points, with puffy clouds hovering over the tips.

Corgan wondered where they'd be able to land, because the tall cliffs seemed to drop straight down into the sea—they were solid rock, with no soil or green growth on them. He could see no beaches where they could pull the *Tuli* ashore. And now, still far from shore, the waves were starting to get choppy.

"We'll have to circle the island until we find a good place," Royal said, turning his head so Ananda could hear him and then pass the message back to Corgan.

"There! Look over there!" Ananda shouted. "Behind that curving jut of rock or coral or whatever it is. Looks like it's a lagoon. If we can steer around the arm of rock, we can pull up onshore. At least it seems low and level there."

Going straight ahead was one thing—the three of them had worked that out amazingly well. Trying to spiral the *Tuli* around a long, circling arm of rock was riskier. The *Tuli* kept revolving aimlessly until Corgan jumped into the water and pushed it from behind, guiding it toward the pebble-covered beach.

Seven

Corgan said, "We'll divide the work. Royal, go catch some fish."

"You're giving orders now?" Royal protested. "I thought I was supposed to be captain."

"Yeah, you are—on the sea. I get to be captain on land."

"What about me?" Ananda asked. "What do I get to be captain of? The sky?"

Corgan thought fast and came back with, "You'll be the goddess of fire, Ananda. Wherever we go, you'll make fire."

She tilted her head to consider that. "Okay, I accept. I'll be the fire builder. Just don't think that makes me the cook, too. I don't like cooking."

"I'll cook," Royal volunteered.

"Agreed. While you two are busy, I'm gonna climb to high ground and try to locate Hiva Oa from here," Corgan told them. "It'll help if we know which direction to take tomorrow. On my way back I'll bring some fruit and water." Though Ua Pou's spires were bare rock, the hills between them grew thick with vines, tree roots, and foliage, the same as in the jungles of Nuku Hiva. Finding fruit would be easy. Grapefruit, mangoes, bananas—he'd pick twice as much as they could eat tonight, because if they didn't find any dogs on this island, tomorrow's voyage to Hiva Oa would be a long one. They'd need food.

Taking the water bag Delphine had given them, Corgan hiked to a high pass, enjoying the feel of ground beneath his feet after all those hours on water. Sweating from the steep climb, he stopped between two towering rock spires. The sun was setting—that was west. Hiva Oa would be south and east, more east than south, but he couldn't see very far. Giving up, he trekked down the hill and through the jungle again, pausing often to listen for the sound of splashing water. From time to time he heard another sound, a faint one. Maybe an animal sound! Dogs? Would they get lucky and find wild dogs right here, on their first try? But the noises he heard were too indistinct to recognize.

A waterfall noise, though, kept getting louder. Breaking through the thickly vined trees, he found it—a cascade thirty meters high, splashing into a pool at the bottom, sparkling in the low rays of the evening sun. It looked so inviting that he dived into the pool for a swim, washing off all the salt that had stuck to his skin from the sea. He gulped the fresh water and then filled the water bag, but when the sun started dipping lower, he knew he'd better get back to the others.

Picking his way through the tropical rain forest that was even more tangled than the one on Nuku Hiva, he suddenly stopped short. He'd almost tripped over something.

A dead animal. A wild boar. Female and not full grown, with its hind hoof stuck in a crevice in the rock. It must not have been able to free itself and died of thirst. Most likely it hadn't been dead very long, because it didn't smell bad. Maybe those animal sounds he'd heard were the last faint, dying squeals of the boar. Corgan considered dragging it back to the fire for the three of them to eat but decided against it since he couldn't be entirely sure how long it had been dead. Flies buzzed all around the boar's body, swarming especially over the eyes.

Grabbing fruit from the trees as he went, he wound his way through the thinning rain forest until he caught sight of Ananda's fire. There was Royal, holding two sticks with fish on them over the flames, while Ananda swung the machete, chopping breadfruit into pieces.

"I saw a dead boar back there," Corgan announced as he set down the water bag.

"How long was it dead?" Royal asked, reaching for a drink.

"I don't know. Couldn't be too long. In this climate things rot pretty fast."

"Want to show me?" Royal asked, getting up and handing the water bag to Ananda. "I could probably tell when it died."

"Not now. It's too dark inside the trees. I'll show you in the morning."

"You know, that presents an excellent possibility, Corgan," Ananda declared. "A dead boar, I mean. If there are wild dogs on this island, they'll follow the scent and start feasting on it tonight. Tomorrow morning if there are tooth marks on the bones, we'll know there are dogs here. And if there aren't . . ."

"Smart girl," Royal said. "Good thinking."

Fish, fruit, and fresh water made a satisfying meal. Royal had chopped piles of banana leaves for them to sit on, and later to lie on, because the beach was made of oddly marked pebbles not nearly as comfortable as sand.

Corgan quietly watched the others, noticing how firelight reflected on their faces and bodies. All three of them, he realized, had similar coloring. Royal's skin had the ruddiness of dark bronze, and when he smiled, his teeth shone white against his brown face. Although his hair was thick and black like Corgan's, it had curls sleek from coconut oil.

Long ago Ananda's grandparents had been software engineers from a country called India, Corgan knew. Before the devastation they'd come to what was then the United States to take classes. Her other grandparents were American Indians from a tribe called Lakota. From one or two or all of those grandparents she'd inherited skin more dusky than bronze. Her eyes were so dark that the pupils seemed to melt into the irises, and her glossy black hair hung straight down, except when she walked—then it swung rhythmically around her shoulders. Corgan had always known Ananda was pretty; now, seeing her with flame flickering in her eyes and with her lips slightly parted, he realized just how beautiful she was.

Royal's coloring came from Samoa, and Ananda's from her mixed ancestry, but Corgan had no idea where his own brown eyes and black hair had originated—except in a test tube. What kind of genetic legacy did he have? None. No ancestors had come before him. His life started from that first moment in the laboratory when random cells were fused to create him.

His musing ended abruptly when Ananda threw more sticks onto the fire and said, "I wish I knew what Cyborg was doing now."

"Probably the same thing we're doing," Corgan answered. "Sitting beside a fire and watching sparks fly into the night."

"Did you ever have any boyfriends before Cyborg, Ananda?" Royal asked.

She stirred the fire before she answered, "Well, I was sort of interested in Corgan, but only when we met in virtual reality while he was still in Wyoming."

"And then you met the real Corgan and that finished it, right?" Royal laughed at his own joke, slapping his thick thigh in mirth.

Ananda smiled a little at that but said, "No, it was just . . . Cyborg told me that Corgan was hopelessly in love with Sharla, so I didn't think I had a chance. Besides, Cyborg was so . . . so . . ."

"So so what? What does Cyborg have that I don't?" Corgan asked, only half in jest.

"Mmmm, he just knows how to say things to make me feel good."

"Didn't Corgan say nice things to you?" Royal asked.

This time Ananda laughed out loud. "Corgan once complimented me because I didn't sweat too much for an athlete. That's the best he could do."

Royal chuckled, but then he admitted, "Sounds like something I'd say. I'm pretty dumb around girls too."

"Hey, speak for yourself, I wouldn't say I'm dumb exactly," Corgan objected. "I just haven't had much experience. Until two years ago I'd never met a real, live girl. Only virtual ones."

Looking dreamy as the firelight's shadows moved across her face, Ananda said, "Cyborg is not only sweet, he's intellectual."

"Hmp!" Royal countered. "I'd have thought a girl like you

would want a guy who's big and strong in the body, not just in the brain."

"Why? Do you think I'm weak in the brain? Just because I'm the strongest female alive doesn't mean I'm mentally impaired. And Cyborg is no weakling in body either."

"No, no, I didn't mean anything like that!"

Corgan was enjoying this, watching Ananda get indignant while Royal squirmed.

Ananda went on, "I met Cyborg and I loved him right away, but he kept growing older because he was designed to mature rapidly—you know, two years older every month. And then he got Lockered and that stopped his premature aging, but now I'm growing up and he'll stay sixteen forever. Which . . . might . . . become a problem," she finished weakly.

"It won't, Ananda, because we have the Locker," Corgan assured her. "Whenever you decide you want to spend the rest of your life at a certain age, we'll Locker you. I know you probably have bad feelings about the Locker because I traded Demi for it, but it can help you if you let it."

"I'm . . . reconciling to that," she answered. "The part about Demi."

As the fire burned lower, the three lay on the beach far enough apart that they wouldn't accidentally touch one another in their sleep. Judging by the sound of his breathing, Royal must have fallen asleep in minutes. Corgan lay awake, listening to the waves. They rolled in rhythmically, slapping at the shore, and then rolled back out again. He heard other sounds he couldn't recognize, but they didn't seem to be animal sounds—more like the calls of seabirds. He'd noticed terns flying low over the waves, darting down to catch fish in their beaks. Terns didn't caw or cry; they squeaked to communicate, not loud enough to keep him awake.

And then he heard Ananda softly murmur, "I'm sorry for everything I said to you, Corgan, when you left Demi on the space station."

"Forget it." It was over, and they needed to put it behind them.

"No, I've been thinking about it, and I really did act like a witch after I lost Demi. But now you're trying to make that up to me, so I owe you."

"You don't owe me anything, Ananda," he told her. If they could find a dog and clone Demi, that might distract him from brooding over Sharla—he'd come to Nuku Hiva to reunite the bond they'd once shared, but it wasn't working. The problem was inside himself, he realized. Every time he and Sharla nearly connected, painful memories crept back to obsess him, so that he was the one who pulled back.

"Yes, I do owe you. I owe you the truth," Ananda said. She came closer to him, leaning over him to announce, "We haven't been honest with you—Cyborg, Sharla, or I."

"Not honest? What are you talking about?"

"Uh . . ." She paused, then in a low voice admitted, "We didn't tell you this, but Cyborg has been in touch with Brigand, doing that psychic connection thing they have where they can read each other's thoughts."

Corgan bolted upright to face her in the flickering firelight. "Are you serious! Why didn't *Cyborg* tell me?" he demanded, feeling the heat of betrayal rise through his core. "Why's he doing that thing with Brigand?"

Defensively Ananda answered, "Don't be mad, Corgan.

It's not like he can turn the connection on and off—he can't control it if Brigand wants to telepath him. Anyway, Cyborg always feels like he's pulled between you and Brigand in a tug-of-war. You're his best friend, but Brigand is his clone-twin." She hurried on, "And he says he doesn't want to influence your choices about staying on Nuku Hiva. He says he . . . he's . . . *beholden* to you because you took him to the space station and made a deal to have him Lockered, and that's what saved his life."

Corgan cried, "You better tell me what's going on between Brigand and Cyborg!"

"Turn it down a notch, Corgan," she hissed. "We don't want to wake Royal. He doesn't know any of this."

"Tell me right now," Corgan threatened, "or I'll yell so loud they'll hear me on Nuku Hiva."

Hesitant, Ananda settled a few more sticks on the fire, making it blaze briefly. Then she said in a rush, "Here's the story. Brigand is forcing Thebos to build another antigravity spaceship exactly like the *Prometheus*. He plans to bring it to Nuku Hiva, then after he destroys you, he'll take Sharla and Cyborg back to Florida."

Corgan almost laughed, but it turned into a snort of derision. "What a joke! Brigand couldn't even fly the Harrier jet without crashing it through the dome. He'd *really* wreck a spacecraft like the *Prometheus*."

"He doesn't plan to pilot it," Ananda said. "He's going to make Thebos both build it and pilot it here."

"Thebos fly a spacecraft!" Corgan stared at her in astonishment. "Thebos is ancient! He couldn't even climb inside the *Prometheus* back in the Flor-DC—I had to install the monitors myself. No, this is just too lunatic. If Brigand forced him to do that, it could kill Thebos!"

"Calm down," Ananda said, putting her hand on his mouth. "This whole thing might not be real. Cyborg says maybe it's just a threat—just Brigand's strategy to get you back to Florida."

"But what if it *is* real? I can't let that happen! Thebos is my . . ." He searched for the right word—*teacher, surrogate grandfather, mentor*—"My friend!" he said. "I have to get back to the Flor-DC to see if he needs help."

Ananda's voice rose, but not enough to wake Royal. "Hey, you're going too fast here! You said we'd hunt for a dog to clone Demi. You promised."

"Yeah." Corgan crossed his arms over his chest and bit his lip, his thoughts whirling. "You're right. I promised." That was supposed to be his good deed to atone for leaving Demi on the space station. Trying to sort it out, he said, "How about here's a deal—we'll hunt for dogs on this island tomorrow, and if we don't find any, we'll go back to Nuku Hiva."

Immediately she shot back, "Here's *my* deal. If we don't find any dogs tomorrow, we try one more island, and if we can't find any there, *then* we'll go back."

Corgan thought it over for six and nine-tenths seconds and then said, "Done." They touched fists. "Now go to sleep."

Maybe she did, maybe she didn't, but at least she moved away. Corgan stayed awake for a long time, worrying. Could Brigand be serious about the threat to fly to Nuku Hiva? Or maybe, as Cyborg suspected—or at least Ananda said he suspected—it was only a tactic to make Corgan return to the

Flor-DC, where Brigand could waste him. Both clone-twins had been created as strategists, so they were way better than Corgan at playing mind games. But he couldn't take any chances. If there was a possibility the threat was a real one, he'd have to save Thebos from Brigand's insanity.

What bothered him especially was the secrecy. The three people he valued most had shut him out of the loop. Cyborg he could almost understand—Brigand was his clone-twin. And Ananda always sided with Cyborg. But Sharla!

Sharla's silence felt like just one more betrayal.

Eight

Morning came, amazingly beautiful. The clouds in the eastern sky changed from the hue of cherries to oranges to lemons as Ua Pou's high peaks caught the rising sun. A calm breeze flowed over Corgan's bare chest and dried his hair, damp from humidity. For a little while he lay unmoving, not wanting to get up and leave this sense of comfort that wrapped him.

When he finally turned to see if the others were awake, he found Royal crouched above the nearly dead fire, stirring the ashes with a stick. Royal was frowning, his dark brows lowered over narrowed eyes.

Rising, Corgan asked him, "What's wrong?"

"A dream," Royal answered. "My grandfather told me there's trouble ahead."

Although Corgan didn't altogether believe in these dreams, he felt his skin jump. "What kind of trouble?"

"He didn't explain. He just said there's too many ghosts on this island."

"Then, we should get out of here," Corgan said. "Get moving, Ananda. We need to load the *Tuli* and take off."

"Not till after we hunt for dogs," Ananda reminded him. "First we'll check the dead boar."

"Oh, yeah. I hope I can find it. It was getting dark last

night when I saw the body, and I'm not sure how to get back there now."

"Maybe you left footprints," Royal said.

As they climbed across jungle foliage and swept through vines, Royal spotted signs that Corgan would totally have missed—not just footprints, but broken twigs and small depressions left in the dirt where Corgan had kicked rocks out of the way. Far in the distance they could hear, faintly, the waterfall. But there were other noises too, the ones Corgan had noticed the evening before but couldn't identify, and those were the sounds that grew louder—an odd kind of chirping, or squeaking, high and shrill, like an unoiled hinge. The farther they went, the clearer the sounds became, with enough tiny variations in pitch to hint that there had to be more than one whatever-it-was making the noise.

Then they broke through to the boar's body, or what was left of it.

"Oooh! It's awful!" Ananda cried out, turning away.

Only the boar's head was visible, chewed down to the skull, with the eyes and jowls and hide all gone. What was left was covered with mounds of undulating, heaving pink flesh. At Ananda's cry, heads flew up and dozens of pairs of glimmering eyes stared at them.

"Rats!" Royal stated, backing up.

"They can't be rats," Corgan argued. "They're too big. They're as big as cats, and they're naked. No hair at all. They're . . ." And then it hit him, and he knew what he was seeing, knew how this ugly mass of alien membrane had happened. "They're mutations!"

"I don't care what they are," Ananda quavered, "they're horrible!"

A few of the rats turned toward them, forming a row, rising up on their hind legs, their front legs waving. Others did the same, reminding Corgan of the New Rebel Troops that had guarded Brigand back in the Flor-DC, but these vermin were not guarding a leader, they were guarding their meal. Their heads moved from side to side, their mouths uttered a strange chittering sound, and their eyes shone a peculiar green as they peered at the three humans who had disturbed them. Some of the rats still chewed, their mouths moving rapidly up and down, and their long front teeth protruding over narrow jaws. But what made them look so obscene, so alien, was the hairless skin, soft and pink and supple and . . . almost human, covering their swollen bodies.

"The plague that wiped out the people on this island must have spread to the rats," Corgan said. "Instead of dying, the rats mutated."

"Maybe they grew so big because they ate all the people who died of the plague," Ananda said, shuddering. "Maybe that's why they mutated. If there were any wild dogs here, the rats probably ate them, too. Let's get out of here before they decide we're food and come after us."

"They can't run as fast as we can," Royal said.

"How do you know that?" Corgan countered. "Even ordinary rats run pretty fast, and when these ones mutated, they might have turned extra swift."

Royal considered that and nodded. "Then, let's just start backing off. Nice and slow. Keep staring them in the eye."

"Which eye? There're about a thousand eyes," Ananda gasped as the chittering grew louder.

"No, only about a hundred eyes. You move, I'll stare," Royal told her. "Get behind me and back up a step at a time."

For one whole minute and forty and a half seconds it became a staring contest, Corgan and Royal in front, Ananda behind them, as the rat chorus rose in volume. Suddenly the first rat darted forward, followed by another, then half a dozen, then—

"Run!" Royal yelled.

The three of them raced through the jungle, barely ahead of the rat pack. When they reached the beach, Corgan shouted, "Load the boat. I'll hold them off."

Luckily the fire still had a few live coals. Corgan grabbed two sticks from the cinders, hoping the ends would keep burning, and began swinging them in an arc in front of the rats as they poured through the trees onto the beach. "Hurry up!" he yelled. "Get the canoe into the water!"

One of the rats rushed forward to lunge at Corgan's leg. He kicked it and sent it flying across the beach, where it smashed against a rock. Immediately a group of other rats ran toward their fallen comrade and began eating it.

Another rat leaped for Corgan's face, but he dodged it. When the rat flew past his shoulder, he whirled and stomped on it, cracking its skull beneath his foot. More and more rats crept forward, some cautious, others darting at him. Thanks to the fast reflexes he'd been bred with, he managed to kick them out of the way as if this were a deadly game of Go-Ball, but the hordes seemed to increase in number. Their jibbering rose to squeals so loud Corgan almost missed Royal's command, "Get in the boat!"

"Fast!" Ananda screamed.

He turned and raced toward the waves. As he splashed through the water, he remembered having heard somewhere that rats could swim, but when he turned to look, he saw that the mutant rats were still onshore, feasting on their dying and dead mates that littered the beach.

Waves kept pulling the *Tuli* away from shore as Corgan struggled to swim toward the canoe. When he finally got close enough, Royal reached out with the paddle. Corgan grabbed it and Royal dragged him in.

"The water bag!" Corgan gasped, heaving himself over the side of the boat. "I never refilled the water bag."

"Don't worry. We have the coconuts and fruit," Ananda told him. "We won't dehydrate."

Corgan wasn't sure. "It depends on how far we have to go and how much we sweat," he argued.

"Well, I'd rather be thirsty than become rat food," Ananda shot back. "They were the most hideous things I've ever seen in my life! Just be thankful they didn't eat us while we were on the beach last night."

"At least it's over," Royal said, "the trouble my grandfather warned me about."

Corgan hoped that was right, but trouble seemed to be surrounding him. "Check the sun," he said. "That's east. We're supposed to be going southeast to Hiva Oa." Shaken by the rat invasion, they were paddling out of sync, plus the wind had risen and the seas were choppy enough to push them off course. He had a feeling that more trouble might lie ahead.

They had to paddle twice as hard as they had on the first leg of their mission, and Ananda frequently stopped paddling to bail. The trip to Ua Pou had been helped by clear weather that let them see the island as they pulled toward it, but today the skies were cloudy. No matter how hard Corgan peered in what he thought was the right direction, he saw no sign of a land mass.

So deal with it, he told himself. *Think! Figure things out!* They'd better manage to reach Hiva Oa in ten hours or less. If they didn't, they'd be floundering around in darkness, and that would mean very big trouble. They were heading southeast, but southeast covered a lot of territory. Though Hiva Oa was supposed to be the biggest island in the chain, compared with the vastness of the Pacific Ocean it was no bigger than a single seashell on a wide beach.

The sun stayed mostly behind the clouds but slid out often enough as the day wore on that Corgan could count off the hours fairly accurately. With each passing hour his back hurt more, and the muscles in his arms started to burn. Most of all he felt thirsty, and they had no fresh water.

"Here," Ananda said, turning around to hand him a grapefruit. "Suck the juice out of it. That'll help with the thirst. Then eat the rest of it. We have plenty of coconuts, too, so we should be fine. Maybe."

"Maybe," Corgan echoed.

More hours passed and the seas got even choppier. Corgan's throat felt chokingly dry, and his arms were so numb he had to stop paddling, if only for a minute. He tried to hide it from Ananda, who seemed as energized as ever, but when she turned and saw him resting his paddle crosswise on the *Tuli,* she told him, "Go ahead, take a break." Before he could argue, she turned back and began to churn the water like a propeller.

One more hour went by. The three of them were paddling more vigorously now because they knew they needed to reach land before dark. Suddenly Ananda shouted, "Look over there! I see it! It's the island! We're gonna make it! Woo-hoo!"

"We're not there yet," Royal said grimly. "And we're taking in a lot more water than we ought to. These waves keep getting higher."

"Okay, you guys paddle and I'll bail again," Ananda decided, and started scooping water out of the canoe so fast the fish must have thought a squall had hit them.

Seeing their destination should have made paddling easier, since it let them know where they were heading. Yet the swelling tide built the surf higher and swifter, and as the sun dropped nearer to the horizon, the island didn't seem to get any closer. Soon they'd need to pick out a landing spot. "Do you want me to bail for a while?" Corgan asked Ananda.

"No, I'm fine, I bail and then I paddle." She'd turned toward him, and maybe that's why neither of them saw what was coming.

Royal did. He yelled out in fear just as the big wave hit.

Nine

The wall of water wrapped around the three of them like the palm of a giant hand, lifting the *Tuli* until it overturned and tossed them into the roiling waters. The force of the rogue wave thrust Corgan so deep he scraped his chest on the sea bottom. He fought upward, rising toward the dark shape floating above his head—that had to be the *Tuli*. When he broke through the surface, he found Ananda clinging to the upside-down canoe, her wet hair pasted across her face, her eyes wide with fright. "Where's Royal?" she gasped.

Fighting for breath, Corgan hung on to the canoe with one arm while he turned around to search . . . and search . . . scanning 360 degrees of sea surface . . . and then doing it over again. There was no sign of Royal.

Ananda cried, "Find him, Corgan!"

Before she'd finished speaking, Corgan plunged into the sea, circling underwater with his eyes wide open even though the salt stung them, swimming through hordes of small silvery fish, hunting for any sign of movement. He burst upward for air and dived again, panic rising in him because twice before he'd done this very same thing, tried desperately to rescue a drowning friend—Cyborg.

His mind filled with an image of Delphine's accusing face. *Don't let her be right!* he prayed. *I can't lose Royal!* Holding his breath until his lungs grew tortured, he glided deep across the dimly lit ocean bottom. The waves that crashed toward shore rolled backward again, trying to suck him out to sea, but he fought the undertow until he saw a shadowy figure suspended above him. Face down, arms outstretched, hanging there motionless except for the swaying of the current—*was he dead?*

Corgan shot upward to wrap his arms around the body, then hauled Royal through the waves to the *Tuli*. "Pull him across the hull of the boat," he panted to Ananda. "Lay him crosswise. Facedown. No! Keep his face out of the water—if he's not dead, he's got to puke up the seawater he swallowed."

As Ananda jerked Royal's head up by the hair, Corgan saw a cut across his forehead where the canoe must have hit him when it flipped; blood ran down Royal's cheek and into the waves. *If he's bleeding, he must be alive,* Corgan hoped as he reached across Royal's inert body, pumping hard against his broad, unmoving back—two, three, four times, a dozen times—until, "He's puking," Ananda shouted, and then, "He's breathing."

Corgan allowed himself eight and a half seconds to feel huge relief before he was forced to focus on the next target: the shore. How far was it, and how much longer could they count on the faint daylight? Only then did he notice for the first time that the outrigger was gone. "What happened to the outrigger?" he called to Ananda.

"I think it broke off and floated away."

The outrigger was the pole that kept the canoe balanced. Without it they could never make it all the way back to Nuku Hiva.

"Keep holding Royal, Ananda," he told her, "and keep his head up out of water. I'm going down again."

"Why?"

"Everything we had is gone—the food, the tools, the outrigger. I'll try to find the tools—we'll need them to make a new outrigger. And paddles." They could survive without the fishing nets and water bag if they had to, but with no tools they might never get off Hiva Oa.

On his first dive he found the machete. If it turned out to be the only tool he found, it would at least let him repair the boat. When he rose empty-handed from his second dive, he noticed that Royal was awake but groggy. Royal managed to say, "You saved me."

Corgan shook his head. "You can thank me later."

"We're drifting toward shore," Ananda said. "Should we try to turn over the canoe and get Royal inside?"

"No! Just leave it capsized and hang on to it the way it is. And hang on to that machete, too, Ananda. I'm going back down."

"Don't take too long! We need to get Royal to dry land!"

He barely heard her last words before he dived again. The tools should have sunk right beneath the spot where the canoe capsized. By great good fortune both the hatchet and the cattle prod lay on the ocean bottom less than two meters apart. "Done!" he said when he reached the surface again, holding the tools in one hand. "Let's go!" He was winded enough that it would have felt good just to hang on to the overturned *Tuli* as it rocked in the waves, but there was no time to rest. He and Ananda started kicking the canoe toward shore.

Royal was dead weight, but the inrushing tide gave them an advantage. *Don't let us crash, don't let us crash,* Corgan kept praying. Clinging to the canoe, they rose and fell with the ocean swells, carried forward by a momentum so powerful that Corgan felt as helpless as Royal. He watched in fear as the waves in front of him broke into a spray of white foam against rocks that lined the beach. Each curling wave seemed to have a life of its own, as individual and distinct as the mountain spires on Ua Pou, but unlike the unmoving spires, the waves moved unpredictably. All Corgan could do was grasp the upside-down *Tuli* with one hand and try to keep hold of the tools with the other hand, hoping that Ananda had a good grip on both the canoe and Royal.

In the fading light he could see a flat beach ahead between mounds of rock, but the waves seemed to be carrying them more toward the rocks than the beach. "Kick harder!" he yelled to Ananda. "Go to the right! There's sand over there."

That Ananda! Her strength and instincts were amazing. Corgan couldn't have done it alone, but the two of them working together maneuvered the canoe toward the beach. Suddenly the waves became smaller and gentler, lapping at the beach instead of crashing. "You take Royal, I'll get the canoe," Corgan told Ananda as their feet touched bottom. At that moment sheets of rain began to blow across them, the drops hitting so hard they pockmarked the water's surface.

Ananda lifted Royal and carried him, his legs dragging, while Corgan shoved the *Tuli* from behind, leaving grooves in the sand as he pushed it high enough that the waves wouldn't pull it back. Then the real squall hit, dumping a deluge onto the shore.

Corgan took twenty-three and a fraction seconds to flip the boat right side up, wanting to catch rainwater inside it so they'd have something to drink, since the darkness was now nearly complete. The rain hit so hard it stung his skin, and it felt good, that rain. He stood with his arms hanging at his sides and with his face upturned to it, letting it wash away the sea that still clung to his body.

"You're safe now," Ananda told Royal as she held him in her arms, trying to support him upright. "We need a fire, Corgan. Royal feels so cold!"

"A fire? How am I supposed to build a fire in this storm?" Corgan started to tell Ananda she should be glad Royal was alive and not demand impossible things, but then he saw how bedraggled she looked. Her green LiteSuit hung torn and sagging, her knuckles had been scraped raw, and seaweed stuck to her long, straggling hair. She must be exhausted after their ordeal, yet she kept trying to help Royal.

He picked up the machete and said, "I'll get some fruit we can eat."

"Don't go too far," she warned. "It's getting dark, and I don't want you to get lost. We need you, Corgan."

"I'll be back soon," he told her.

In spite of the pouring rain and the near darkness, picking fruit was as easy on Hiva Oa as it had been on Ua Pou or Nuku Hiva. All the Isles of Hiva grew lush and heavy with tropical fruit. Finding driftwood that had washed high on the beach was easy too. When the rain stopped, he'd maybe try to build a fire, although he wasn't too hopeful it would work.

After an hour the rain did stop. By then the driftwood he'd gathered was completely soaked. "It won't work," he told

Ananda. "The spark from the cattle prod isn't like a flame—it's just an electric jolt. I can light things with it only if there's something dry and fuzzy to catch the sparks."

"Isn't there any other way to build a fire?" Ananda asked, worried.

"Not here. Not now. Not without lighters or hot coals, but even if we had those, we don't have any dry wood. At least we don't need a fire for cooking—we have bananas and mangoes."

"It isn't food I'm worrying about," Ananda said. "It's Royal."

He could see what she meant. Royal was sitting up, hunched over and shivering. "Maybe if he ate . . . ," Corgan suggested, but Royal answered, "Don't want to eat."

There was nothing to cover him with to keep him warm, nothing but seaweed to press against his bleeding forehead. Their clothes were wet—Corgan's jeans and tapa cloth shirt, Ananda's LiteSuit, Royal's shirt and cutoff pants. Corgan's shoes were so soaked that they squished when he walked, but luckily all three of them still had their shoes.

"I'm gonna cut some palm fronds so at least we'll have something to lie on," Corgan told them. "Best thing we can do is get some sleep, and when we get up in the daylight, we'll try to figure out how bad off we are. It's too dark to tell anything right now."

"Grandfather warned me," Royal muttered.

Corgan had gone only a few meters when he heard footsteps as Ananda caught up to him. "Listen," she said, "I think Royal's pretty sick. Remember, he's just an ordinary guy. He's strong, but he's not genetically enhanced like you and me. It's up to us to take care of him."

"Okay. But I don't know what else to do."

"I'll let you know." And then she was gone, hurrying back to Royal.

After Corgan had chopped palm fronds and arranged them under the trees, he called out, "We'll sleep up here where the waves won't reach us."

"I'm coming." Ananda lifted Royal to his feet and half led, half carried him to where Corgan waited. Still shivering, Royal sat on the fronds in the same crouching position. "Why is it so cold?" he asked. Corgan and Ananda exchanged glances. The night was wet but not really cold, maybe seventy-five or seventy-eight degrees Fahrenheit.

"Lie down, Royal," Ananda told him. "I'll lie next to you to keep you warm."

Standing silently, Corgan watched Ananda arrange Royal on the ground. Then she stretched out beside him, curling up to him with her arm across his chest. She glanced up at Corgan and said, "You too. Lie down on his other side."

"Me?"

"Do you see anyone else around here?" she asked. "Don't just stand there. Get down beside us."

Awkwardly Corgan settled himself onto the fronds. "Closer," Ananda told him. "We have to use our own body heat to keep Royal warm. Closer! Put your arm across him."

Corgan sucked in his breath. This was really weird.

Still shivering, Royal groaned softly, and Ananda wiggled even nearer to him. Corgan lay on his back with his right arm across Royal's chest, but that felt awkward. Fighting the urge to get up and move away, he turned on his side to face Royal and put his left arm across him, surprised at how much Royal was shaking with cold. Corgan lay stiffly, totally uncomfortable—not because he was lying on the ground, but because he was lying so close to another human being, and it was a male.

The only other person Corgan had been this physically close to, ever, was Sharla. She was the first person he'd ever touched, back in the Wyo-DC, two years ago, just before the start of the Virtual War, and the only person he'd ever touched body to body, although never very often or very entirely—no, wait! That wasn't true. There was one other person.

Corgan's wrestling match with Brigand in that final fight in the Flor-DC had to be considered close physical contact—Brigand with his oiled, bare torso, his powerful arms, his head butting Corgan under the chin. That was human contact, but it had been fueled by rage.

Now, though, lying uncomfortably beside the shivering Royal, Corgan had to fight the impulse to move away. He forced himself to stay still, to fill his thoughts with over-whelming gratitude that Royal had lived and not drowned. Delphine would go totally mental if anything happened to Royal. Or to any of them.

As the minutes passed, Corgan became aware of the night sounds. Some of them were the same as on Ua Pou—the squeaking noises made by the seabirds, the terns. He strained his ears to hear if there were any other squeaks that might be coming from mutant rats, but heard nothing like that. Yet there was another sound, a different sound. Wide awake now, he tried to identify it.

An animal sound, he was pretty sure. A howl—but different from the midnight yowling of the few feral cats on Nuku Hiva. This was far away, rising and falling, too faint to recognize. Whatever was making the sound wasn't close enough to be a threat.

His right arm curled under his head, Corgan tried to stay awake to figure out what he might be listening to, but sleep once again captured him, and he heard only the sound of his dreams.

Ten

The first words Royal spoke when he woke up were, "My grandfather came to me again last night."

"Wait, how are you feeling?" Ananda asked. Although Royal's forehead was swollen, his cut had stopped bleeding, and he sat up straight, not slumped over.

"I'm feeling good. Don't you want to hear what my grandfather said?"

"Yeah. Sure we do." So many things had come true, like yesterday's disasters, that Corgan found himself intensely curious about any new predictions. "Tell us."

"Grandfather said . . ." Royal paused, glancing at both of them, building suspense. "He said everything will be tranquil when two Royals take me where my heart will lie."

"Two Royals?" Ananda questioned. "What does that mean?"

"I don't know. He didn't explain."

Take me where my heart will lie. Could that mean a grave? A watery grave? It made Corgan a little uneasy, but no matter how much they quizzed Royal, he just shrugged his broad shoulders and said they'd have to wait and see.

They didn't have long to wait. While they ate pineapple for breakfast, things began to wash up onto the shore. First, all three paddles swept up onto widely separate sections of the beach, and Corgan ran from one to the other picking them up. Then came the bag Sharla had woven from rope to hold the dog if they caught one; it landed almost at their feet. After that the tapa cloth shirt Delphine had sewn for Ananda and then the water bag—they swept in and out on the waves until Ananda waded in and grabbed them.

"Do you see the outrigger?" Corgan wanted to know.

"No."

"Not to worry," Royal told them. "We can make another outrigger. There's plenty of wood."

"Right. We've got about everything we need now," Corgan said, "except fresh water—there's hardly any water left in the canoe. Will you be okay, Royal, if Ananda and I look for some?"

Royal nodded. "Maybe I'll take a nap and get an update from my grandfather." He grinned to let them know he was joking, then gave them a small wave of his hand.

As they explored the landscape, Ananda and Corgan saw that Hiva Oa had the same rugged volcanic peaks as Ua Pou and Nuku Hiva, with a wall of high rock surrounding the shores that circled the bay. "Best thing to do is get to some high ground where we can look around for a stream," Corgan told her. She followed him up a hill that wasn't much of a climb compared with the peaks farther away. Near the top of the hill they noticed several stone blocks fitted together into a low mound, with mortar between the blocks, holding them together. Corgan had seen something sort of like it on Nuku Hiva—the tomb of a long-dead cannibal chief. Would this turn out to be another chief's tomb?

When they reached it, they discovered a large, round

boulder embedded in front between two of the square blocks that made up the structure. "There's writing on the boulder," Ananda said. She traced her finger along the grooves of letters someone had carved into the boulder, letters about twelve milli-meters deep and nine centimeters wide. "*P* . . . *A* . . . *U* . . . *L*," she read. Another line of letters curved beneath the "Paul." "*G* . . ." Ananda's finger stopped as she said, "I can't tell whether this next one is an *A* or a four."

"If it's a name, it's gotta be an *A*," Corgan told her. "*A* . . . *U* . . . *G* . . . *U* . . . *I* . . . *N*. Gauguin. That's a strange name. Wait a minute! I remember that name." He frowned in concentration. "I think . . . Sharla told me, the first time we were on the Isles of Hiva, that some famous artist lived right here on Hiva Oa a long time ago. That was his name. Paul Gauguin. Here's a date under the name, 1903. So okay, so hi, Paul, if you're buried under here, nice meeting you, but we need to find water, then go back to fix the canoe."

"Aren't we searching for dogs? Isn't that why we're here?" Ananda flashed him a sharp look to make sure he wasn't back-ing out.

"Sounds like you want to search," he responded, "even after all the bad things that happened yesterday with the mutated rats and the canoe capsizing. You know, we could have all been killed. Like Delphine said."

"But you promised to search for a dog! And we're here! So we should at least *try* to find one."

Corgan knew it would be smart to pack up and leave before something even more dangerous happened. This ven-ture was too risky, and Corgan was plagued by his need to get back to Florida and save Thebos—if Thebos needed saving.

But Ananda's dark eyes kept searching his face, waiting for his answer. "Look," she said, "if we can't see any dogs on this island, then we'll forget the search and go back to Nuku Hiva. That was the deal. But you have to give it your best try."

"Okay, here's what I think," he told her. "It'll take me at least a day to make a new outrigger for the *Tuli*, or maybe less than that if Royal feels well enough to help me."

She waited expectantly. "I'm listening."

"So how 'bout if Royal and I work on the boat, and you can go on a dog hunt?"

"By myself? What if I find a dog? How can I catch it without any help?"

"With that bag Sharla wove out of rope. That's what it's for, to hold a dog."

"And you expect me to do that by myself—are you serious?" Ananda's stare was disbelieving. "No, you're not. You've got to be joking. If there's a whole pack of dogs, they might attack me. I'll need help. That's not negotiable."

He shrugged, picked up a stone, and threw it toward the bay. "Okay. I respect that. You need my brains and brawn. We'll do it your way."

"Oh, give it a rest about the brains and brawn. I just need another pair of hands," Ananda told him, but she was smiling because she'd won.

After that it didn't take them long to locate a stream, where they rinsed out the water bag and filled it with fresh, clear water. Since there was no waterfall, Ananda knelt beside the stream and bent over it to wash her long hair, while Corgan pretended not to watch her. Though her strength was amazing, she was also graceful, and he had to admit she made a dazzling picture there beside the stream. When she glanced up at him, he looked away quickly, as though he'd been focusing on something else.

That's when he saw it. "Ananda, come look at this," he told her. "Not right here, but downstream a little farther."

She got to her feet, swinging her hair around so the drops flew out in a thin sheet. "What'd you find?"

"Something metal—it looks like a pole."

She reached it before he did, and when she picked it up, she said, "I think it's hollow. It's sealed at both ends." She handed the tube to Corgan. "You open it. There might be something alive in there."

"Oh, come on!" He took it from her, wondering how long the tube had been lying there near the stream. Probably since the inhabitants of Hiva Oa had died off, and that was decades ago. It must have been drenched by the rain that fell almost daily on these islands, and that was why Corgan was having so much trouble prying off either end of the tube: Corrosion had sealed the caps tightly. He picked up a rock and knocked it hard against one of the ends until finally he could unscrew the top.

"What's inside?" Ananda asked. "Anything?"

"Ooh, it's alive, it's a snake!" he teased. "I'm joking." He reached in and pulled out a rolled-up cloth as long as the tube. Tapa cloth? It felt different. "Here, take one side," he told Ananda. "Let's unroll it."

It was rolled from top to bottom—the top was a meter and a half wide—and as they unfurled the cloth, it became longer than it was wide, about two meters in length. "It's a painting!" Ananda exclaimed, and then both of them fell silent.

The picture showed a young man, or he might have been an almost grown-up boy, standing next to a canoe, a dugout canoe with three crosswise boards as seats. In the bay before him rose the tall, wide mound of rock, the same mound the *Tuli* had avoided crashing into the night before. The man-boy looked muscular across the shoulders, and his left arm, too, was well muscled as he raised a coconut shell toward his lips as if to drink from it. He wore nothing but knee-length pants. His skin glowed dark bronze, and his black hair had been cropped close to his head.

"Do you see it?" Ananda breathed.

"Yeah," Corgan answered, nodding. "I see it. Weird."

Except for the short hair, the painting looked exactly like Royal. Exactly!

"Two Royals!" Ananda said softly. "His grandfather said two Royals." For a full minute they stared, unspeaking, as the breeze rattled the painting a bit. The amazing likeness unsettled Corgan, as if his world had tilted ever so slightly. But a new, more important idea hit him, one that dealt with the world the way he liked it—solid and real. Excited, Corgan declared, "This is a major find. Major! Do you realize what we've got here?"

"Art?" she asked.

Corgan half laughed, half scoffed. "Think, Ananda! It's a sail. We just lucked out—we found a sail and the outrigger both at the same time. This tube can be the outrigger."

"You're going to use this beautiful picture as a sail?" Ananda looked incredulous.

"Yeah, why not? What do we need with a painting?"

"It might be by that artist, that Gauguin."

"He died a long time ago. What we could really use is a sail, and this ought to work great."

Corgan began to roll it up again, but Ananda cried, "Wait! Look—there's a dog in the right corner of the picture." It was a smooth-haired, yellow-colored dog, short legged, with a long tail. "Dogs must have lived on this island when the picture was painted. Maybe they're still here!"

They hurried back to the beach, and even before they reached it, Ananda shouted to Royal, "We found Royal Two. Hurry up, Corgan. Show him his double."

After they had unrolled the canvas, Royal stood with his hands on his hips, studying it. "Do I really look like that?" he asked.

"Well . . . yeah!" Corgan exclaimed.

"Only exactly," Ananda confirmed. "It's like you posed for the painting, except it might be more than a hundred years old. It's Royal Two, definitely."

"And not only that, we found this tube we can turn into an outrigger," Corgan told him. "If you're up for it, Royal, we'll attach this to the *Tuli* and then make a mast for the sail."

"What sail, Corgan?" Royal asked, puzzled.

"You're looking at it. The painting will be a great sail. Do you think you can figure out how to make a mast?"

Royal just smiled. "Watch me!"

Eleven

By moonrise the *Tuli* stood ready on the beach, a carefully refurbished craft. Royal had carved a hole in the bottom of the canoe, then inserted a long, thin pole and sealed it with resin from a breadfruit tree. Corgan tied spars across the mast to support the sail, and when the sail was furled in place, they packed all their supplies except for the cowhide water bag and the rope sack.

Ananda leaned over the fire she'd built, cooking a fish Corgan had speared. Raising her eyes, she asked, "I was wondering—did your grandfather say anything about a dog, Royal? It's like everything he tells you comes true. I thought maybe . . ."

"No, Grandfather didn't mention a dog," Royal answered, "but the next dream is only a couple hours away."

In the morning, though, Royal reported that his sleep had been dream-free during the night. "No visits from my grand-father. I guess he already said everything he wanted to say."

All three of them had heard howls during the night, and they discussed which direction the howls had come from. "To the west," Royal said. "You have good eyes, Ananda, but I have good ears." He seemed to have recovered completely from his near drowning. The swelling on his forehead now showed just a bruise, and the cut had scabbed and was healing. Judging from the size of the breakfast he'd eaten that morning, his stomach hadn't suffered any from the ordeal. "Take the cattle prod," he reminded Corgan. "Just in case. I'll carry the rope sack."

"Are you sure you want to come along on this dog hunt?" Corgan asked him.

"I'm sure. I feel good, and there's nothing left for me to do here on the beach."

"You already caught a lot of fish—I'm using some of it for dog bait," Ananda told Royal. "And I've got the machete for a weapon, 'just in case,' like you said."

As they climbed a steep rise, the hot, humid air hung around them like an oven. Sweat dripped from Corgan's hair onto his forehead and into his eyes, making them sting. Mosquitoes swarmed around their heads. "I'm so soaked," Corgan said, "these bugs ought to drown when they bite me."

"You know what I really miss more than anything else?" Ananda asked. "Soap. Back in the Flor-DC I had all these different kinds of soap. They smelled so good . . ."

"Take a sniff of the flowers around here," Corgan suggested. "They smell good too, and if you inhale them, maybe you won't notice my armpits."

"I'll notice. I'm already noticing."

They trekked uphill for another half an hour to the height where foliage started to thin and patches of bare rock showed. Suddenly Ananda exclaimed, "There we go."

"Go where?" Corgan wasn't sure what she meant, since she was pointing at the ground.

"I mean, look down there. See that? It's dog poop. Do you know what this means? There really are dogs here!"

Doubtful, Royal looked from the ground to Ananda and asked, "How can you tell this stuff is from dogs?"

"Royal, I had a dog for four years. I saw dog poop every day—I had to clean it up off the strip of grass Demi was allowed to use for her personal bathroom. Believe me, I know what dog poop looks like. Start checking around."

They didn't hear anything, but they did start to notice other clues—more droppings and a few short, yellowish tufts of hair caught on bushes not more than two feet off the ground. If the hair had come from dogs, the dogs must not be too tall. Maybe they looked like the dog in the painting.

"Stop!" Royal held up his hand. "I heard something in the bushes."

Ananda cautioned, "No, don't stop, keep going. If they're dogs, they'll be running away from us, and we don't want to lose them."

It was hard to hurry because they had to fight the vegetation. Ananda, full of energy, swatted at it with the machete to slice ropelike vines. When at last they broke through the final bit of foliage on the slope, she gasped, "Holy Shiva! Come and see."

On a ledge near the top of the rocky outcrop stood three snarling yellow dogs. They were not really yellow, but a mixture of gold and tan and paler colors all blended together, with darker hair on their snouts around their black noses. As they yipped and growled and snarled all at once, the hair on the backs of their necks rose straight up.

"Female?" Ananda asked. "Can you tell?"

"One of them's male," Corgan said. "I can't get a good look at the others. Got the rope sack ready, Royal?"

"Ready. Go real slow." The three of them crept forward, Royal holding the sack high in both hands while Corgan aimed the cattle prod. Ananda laid down the machete and cautiously reached out toward the three threatened and threatening animals, holding a piece of fish in her hand.

"It's okay, babies," she crooned. "We don't want to hurt you. We're your friends."

The dogs were not large, less than half a meter high at the shoulder, but their teeth looked as if they could tear a nasty chunk out of a person's leg or arm or neck. Recklessly Ananda kept advancing as the dogs backed up, their snarls getting louder, their lips curling back farther, and their jaws opening wider as they tried to intimidate this unknown species coming toward them. In the same soft voice Ananda coaxed them, "Here, look! Here's something nice to eat." She threw a little piece of fish toward them, but the dogs leaped out of the way and began to bark even more furiously.

"We have them trapped," Corgan said. "They can't back up any farther." The ledge the dogs crouched on was no more than two meters square, with a sheer drop on three sides and the slab of wall in back. Not good for the dogs, but not good for Corgan and Ananda and Royal, either. The ledge was a perfect height for canines to launch themselves toward human throats.

"Nice doggies," Ananda murmured. "Want more fish?" When she attempted to throw another piece of fish, two of the dogs leaped off the ledge, hurtling straight at her and knocking her down. As one lunged for her face, Ananda screamed, and Corgan zapped the dog with a charge from the cattle prod while Royal kicked the other one in its belly. Yelping, it sprang past them and ran into the jungle. Both Royal and Corgan wrestled the stunned dog and tied it with rope as Ananda scrambled to get up.

"Are you hurt?" Corgan asked her.

"I'm fine." Crawling to her feet, she cried, "The one you caught in the net . . . male or female?"

"Male," Royal answered.

"Then let him go."

Cautiously Royal began to loosen the rope from around the male dog, which slavered and snarled the whole time. "Move back," he told Corgan and Ananda. When he heaved the dog into the bushes, it ran away howling.

That left just one dog, still on the ledge and crouching forward in a threatening posture, teeth bared, jaws wide, ready to leap. Corgan said, "Go slow. It can't escape."

But he was wrong. With a squeal of fright that sounded almost like a human scream, the dog jumped off the ledge and fell to another far beneath, shrieking in pain as it landed. Ananda shouted, "It's hurt!" Picking her way along a series of narrow ridges that led down the escarpment, she scrambled with both hands and both feet to where the yelping dog lay.

Corgan and Royal followed her down the layered volcanic rock in time to hear her say, "It's female." Though the dog lay writhing on the ledge, it tried to lunge at them, teeth bared, its growls mixed with yelps and whimpers.

"Her back leg is broken. She's biting her own leg," Ananda said. "She doesn't understand why it hurts her so much. And she's terrified. We'll wrap her in the sack to carry her back to the beach."

Luckily the dog was too hurt to move much. They had to dodge her teeth as they threw the sack over her, and she kept fighting, biting through the rope, tangling her teeth and claws as she writhed and kicked her good back leg. Ananda murmured, "I feel terrible. I never meant for the poor thing to get hurt."

"So we should just leave it here," Royal answered. "Why take it with you if it's damaged?"

"Her leg's broken! That doesn't mean she can't be a surrogate mother," Ananda said. "A broken leg doesn't destroy her womb."

"And she's helpless now," Corgan added. "If she can't defend herself, she could get eaten by predators. I'm not gonna leave her here to be some other animal's meal."

It was not exactly a triumphal procession that wound its way through the jungle to the beach, but it was better than being chased by mutant rats.

"I think we should keep her wrapped up," Ananda said. "She's less likely to damage herself that way. I'll tie her into the shirt Delphine made me."

"Use mine," Royal said, pulling it off. "I really don't like wearing a shirt."

As night fell and Ananda held the whimpering dog, by the light of the fire Corgan noticed how worried she looked. "What's wrong?" he asked, dropping to the sand beside her.

"I don't know. I—this is all my fault. Royal nearly drowning, this dog getting hurt." She searched his face with her eyes. "Am I selfish, Corgan? Because right now that's all I've been thinking. If it weren't for me . . ."

He answered, "Not selfish, it's just that you're passionate about things, Ananda. You love really hard. But I know how you feel—I make a lot of decisions that I think are the right ones, and then something goes real wrong." Wryly he added, "And nobody ever lets me forget my mistakes. But you ought to get some sleep—we'll be doing a lot of paddling tomorrow."

"Even with the sail?"

"If we sail and paddle at the same time, we'll get there faster."

The dog whimpered all night long, but Corgan managed to sleep in spite of it. Before dawn he was up, hiking back to the stream to fill the water bag. After they'd loaded the little bit of remaining gear into the *Tuli*, Ananda climbed in and placed the dog between her feet, then Corgan and Royal ran alongside, shoving the craft off the beach and into the waves. They managed to clamber onboard without tipping the canoe or kicking off the new outrigger. As they paddled out past the breakers to calmer waters, and the breeze picked up and filled the sail, Corgan couldn't stop looking at the painting on the canvas. It unsettled him a little, and not in a bad way, it was just sort of . . . mystic.

There were the two Royals. The real Royal leaned to the left and then swung around to lean to the right, maneuvering the spar to guide the sail as the wind blew, and the wind kept blowing exactly where they needed it to. As the sail stirred, the youth in the painting seemed to come alive, to face them with his coconut shell held to his lips as if in a toast to them all. The double image was almost a hallucination—Royal manning the sail, his broad, naked shoulders at the same angle as the shoulders of the look-alike in the painting, and the painted youth bending familiarly toward Royal, then straightening upright as the wind shifted inside the painted sail, ruffling it. *Clones,* Corgan kept thinking. *It's like they're clones. The two Royals.*

Twelve

As they sailed the *Tuli* through the last few waves to reach Nuku Hiva, Corgan felt triumphant. On the shore Cyborg, Sharla, and Delphine stood waiting for them, waving and cheering, and after the *Tuli* landed, Sharla broke away and ran toward Corgan, shouting, "Welcome back!"

Delphine wept as she embraced Royal. Then her expression changed to shock as she cried, "You what! Nearly drowned? Oh, my God! And look at that cut on your head!"

Sharla echoed, "Is that true? Royal nearly *drowned*?"

Corgan felt some of the glory slipping away. "No one drowned," he said defensively. "You can see we're all here and alive."

Not far from them, Cyborg and Ananda were locked in each other's arms, with Ananda whimpering, "I missed you so much!" From the bottom of the canoe the dog howled and barked and yipped, and even the seabirds joined in the general clamor, squalling and squawking overhead.

"Well! You children must be famished," Delphine exclaimed.

"Water first," Corgan told her. "Some of your nice, pure distilled water from the lab would taste like—"

"Like ambrosia," Ananda finished.

"Come on, all of you, into the lab," Delphine urged them.

"I can't wait to hear about your adventures. But my heart's still in a state of shock over Royal nearly drowning! It's what I worried about every moment you were gone."

It was a small procession—the three stay-at-homes dressed in clean clothes, their hair combed and their skin fresh, while the three voyagers straggled behind with their torn, dirty, salt-stained remnants hanging from them, their hair snarled and their bodies full of bruises and scratches and grime. With her usual tact Sharla told Corgan, "You look awful! You must have had a really rough time."

"Thanks."

"We'll slay another fatted calf!" Delphine announced. "We'll roast it over a fire on the beach, and tonight we'll dance in joyful gratitude that all of you are still alive!"

The last thing Corgan wanted was to dance on the beach. But that's what happened hours later, after the travelers were clean and had been fed as much beef and tofu as they could hold. "Sorry. No dancing for me," Corgan told Sharla.

"You're not a lot of fun, Corgan," she answered. "You never learned how to play."

"Sure. I played games all the time. Golden Bees, Go-Ball—"

"Those weren't games, they were training sessions to sharpen your skills. Come on. Dance with me tonight."

"I'll look stupid."

"Who cares? We won't be telecast to a worldwide audience like in the Virtual War. This is just about us. And our friends," she added.

The music wasn't much more than repetitious drumbeats with voices squawking words Corgan could barely understand against a background of instruments he didn't recognize, coming from an audio player like nothing he'd ever seen before.

"It's old," Delphine admitted, "and the music is old too. It's what I grew up with." Surprisingly, Delphine looked lithe and rhythmic as she twisted her hips and waved her arms to the music. The others followed her motions, circling the fire in time to the beat, swaying and weaving. Ananda wore the tapa cloth shirt Delphine had made her and a swath of tapa cloth around her waist, tucked to make a skirt. It was the first time Corgan had seen her amazing legs. Royal had something similar wrapped around his waist, but he informed them loudly and repeatedly that this was definitely not a skirt, it was what Samoan men wore when they danced, especially during a war dance, when they were about to run out and club their enemies.

"Should I be scared?" Cyborg asked, grinning.

"You're not my enemy," Royal answered. "If you were, you'd be scared spitless."

Sharla had on a tapa cloth dress too, short enough to show that her legs rivaled Ananda's. As she danced closer to Corgan, she murmured, "I can tell you're not enjoying this."

"The dancing, no." Looking at the girls, yes.

"It's okay," she said. "Let's go sit on the beach." Moving away quietly so the others wouldn't ask where they were going, they searched out the same spot where they'd talked the night before the *Tuli* voyage. "Are you sore from all that paddling?" Sharla asked Corgan. "Lean back and I'll give you a back rub."

The fire burned high, and Sharla's fingers on Corgan's

back excited him more than soothed him. "So what's next?" she was asking him.

"Maybe I should ask you that, since you know more than you're telling," he answered her. "Ananda said Cyborg and Brigand have been in psychic contact, and she told me what it was about. Why didn't *you* tell me, Sharla? I don't feel good about that. Actually, I'm kinda torqued about it."

Sharla was silent, but her fingers dug a little more deeply into his back. After seven seconds she answered softly, "Ananda wasn't supposed to say anything. You know, Cyborg doesn't start this messaging, Brigand does. He keeps blasting Cyborg's brain with images and thoughts."

"Does Cyborg try to stop him?"

"Yes. No. I don't know. They're clone-twins. Cyborg feels guilty for the way Brigand turned out. I keep trying to tell him it isn't his fault, but he has this guilt. All of us do—we all feel guilty about one thing or another, and it wastes us."

Her fingers dug even deeper into Corgan's back when he said, "You mean all of us except Brigand. I don't think Brigand understands guilt. That whole idea about Thebos building another zero-gravity spacecraft and flying it here—that would kill the old man."

Quietly Sharla said, "It's hard to realize what people can force themselves to do when they're being threatened. And Brigand can be pretty threatening."

"Threaten? Is he *threatening* Thebos?"

"I don't know. If he is, it's probably just a maneuver to bring you back to Florida."

Corgan tried to relax because he didn't want the back rub to end, but he had to wonder how much Ananda had told

Sharla about his plans. After a pause he asked, "Did Ananda mention—"

"That you're all hot to go back? Yes. I heard. And before you ask, the news did not make me happy. Brigand says he wants to kill you. Why go to Florida and give him the chance?"

The answer was so obvious that he was surprised she had to ask. "For Thebos," he repeated. "I already told you—I have to save Thebos."

"I'd rather you saved Corgan," Sharla said, coming around to face him. "Thebos is an old man. You still have your whole life to live. Why do you have to act like a hero?"

He couldn't believe she'd ask that. "Because that's what I was made to be," he declared. "And I haven't been doing so great at it lately. Anyway, this is nonnegotiable. If Brigand's threatening Thebos, I'll have to take my chances with Brigand. It's time we had a showdown anyway. I can't keep running from him."

"Corgan! You can't win against Brigand!" Sharla cried out. "This is a colossally bad idea." She pulled away from him and crouched on the sand facing him. It was dark enough that he could barely see her face, which might have been a good thing because it helped him to remain determined.

"Stay on Nuku Hiva," she begged him. "For a while at least. We'll be together, and you can make some reasonable plans before you go back to Florida. Cyborg will help you plan—he's a strategist."

So tempting! But, "You think Cyborg's going to help me defeat his clone-twin? Sharla—get real. He didn't even tell me he was in touch with Brigand! No, as soon as the Demi clones get implanted, we're out of here."

"I can't change your mind? No matter what *I* want?"

"Afraid not."

This time it was Sharla who walked away, not saying good night, disappearing into the darkness. Why was it that something always happened to spoil things between them? He took a different route and headed for the barn, where he could be alone to think. Alone felt good. He didn't even tell Mendor he was back.

The next day in the lab the dog—Ananda had decided to call her Diva—lay safely confined inside one of the metal cages Delphine had used when she tested newborn calves for transgenic traits. With Ananda holding the dog's mouth tightly closed, Delphine needed only about three minutes to set Diva's leg, splint it, and wrap it tightly with a strip of tapa cloth. "She'll be fine," Delphine assured Corgan as Diva wolfed down the meat Ananda fed her and lapped up a quarter liter of water.

Sharla had come too; she and Delphine hovered over the animal cage talking about cell transfer and DNA and zygotes, things Corgan knew a little about, since he'd helped Delphine and Grimber during all those months when they'd implanted blastocysts into cows to create transgenic calves.

"Do you think it will work?" Sharla asked. Corgan noticed Sharla spoke only to Delphine, ignoring him.

Delphine smiled. "We'll give it a try. It depends on how viable the Demi cells still are. Cloning is tricky business, as you well know, Sharla." Delphine turned away from the cage to ask Corgan, "Is your time-splitting ability still as good as it used to be? It'll be important to implant the cloned cells at exactly the right stage of division."

"I think so." He nodded, and then he brought up something that had been on his mind all during the sail home. "Clones," he began, "they're supposed to be physically identical, right? I know their personalities are different, because everyone keeps reminding me how different Cyborg and Brigand act. But . . . how is it possible for two people to look exactly alike when they aren't related and didn't even live at the same time?"

Delphine gestured to where the painting hung on a wall. "You're talking about that, I assume. About the way it resembles Royal."

"Yes, the painting," Ananda chimed in. "It's like it's Royal's clone."

"The painting is nothing more than a look-alike," Delphine told them. "The odds that the youth in that painting had any genetic connection to Royal are about a trillion to one. Although, actually, at about those odds every human being is genetically related to every other one."

Sharla had gone to stand in front of the painting, examining it closely. "You still haven't given us a guess about why this looks so much like Royal."

"Obviously because Gauguin painted Polynesians," Delphine answered, "although I suspect that this is not an original Gauguin, just a copy. And Royal is a Polynesian, more specifically a Samoan. There's nothing magic or miraculous or ghostly about it. And speaking of ghostly, all these things I've been hearing that Royal says his grandfather told him—pure coincidence."

Raising her voice into lecture mode, she went on, "Life is full of coincidence, kids. Coincidence and chance. You stumbled upon a painting that looks like Royal. That's coincidence. But by chance this same painting that you found worked as a sail and may have saved your life. A lot of people believed, and still believe, that every surprising or unexplained event is determined by God. I don't believe that. I'm a skeptic because I watched the world being destroyed by armies that kept fighting about which god was the right one."

"My grandparents believed in Lord Vishnu," Ananda murmured softly.

"One of many," Delphine said. "But God, in whatever form he or she takes, didn't cause the devastation. People did. Throughout history. A hundred years before this last devastation a tyrant in Europe tried to exterminate all my people for their religious beliefs."

They were very quiet until Sharla asked softly, "Your people, Delphine? Who were your people?"

Delphine sighed and pushed back her thick, curly hair, which tended to creep forward across her cheeks when she wasn't wearing a headband. She didn't really answer Sharla, but said instead, "We've been talking about coincidence and chance. By chance my great-grandparents were helped by some decent people who put themselves at risk. By chance they were hidden on a ship, and they escaped to a country named Brazil. Again by chance, two generations later, my mother survived the devastation and brought me as a baby to the only domed city on the South American continent, and once again by chance I was chosen by the Western Hemisphere Federation to come here to Nuku Hiva to work on the transgenic cattle."

"That last part wasn't chance," Sharla said. "You were chosen because you're brilliant."

Delphine shrugged. "Coincidence and chance. They rule our lives. In the country my great-grandparents escaped from, the word for chance is 'przypadek.' It also translates as 'fortuity, accident, or fortune.'"

All of them had been listening intently to Delphine, trying to understand what she meant. Ananda stood next to the cage, staring down at the dog, perhaps wondering whether chance would favor the birth of a clone of Demi.

Sharla moved hesitantly, pulling her thoughts together. Then she said, "But Corgan and I weren't created by chance, Delphine. We were genetically engineered."

Nodding, Delphine answered, "That's true. You were created to be excellent at certain skills, but that's not all you've done in your lives. Coincidence, chance, and choice—they're very different, and there's only one of the three you get to control. Choice. Many good things happen by choice, like Corgan saving Royal from drowning, which was a brave and heroic rescue. But as Corgan can tell you too, sometimes bad things happen by chance, like Cyborg's hand—if by chance Corgan hadn't left the machete at the side of the pool—"

Corgan felt the hot blood rising to his cheeks. "Don't go there! Please!" he warned her, wanting her to stop. Wouldn't he ever be allowed to forget his careless action that made Cyborg lose his hand? Feeling accused, he hurried out of the lab and by chance nearly ran into Cyborg, who was pushing the levers that controlled his artificial hand.

"This thing isn't working exactly right," Cyborg complained, but Corgan burst out with, "Why didn't you tell me you were in communication with Brigand? I had to find out from Ananda!"

"Whoa, whoa, whoa! What's gnawing on *your* insides?" Cyborg held up both his hands as if to stop Corgan's rush of words. "Okay," Cyborg went on, a flush creeping onto his sun-reddened cheeks, "Ananda told me that she told you, and I guess I should have mentioned it to you before she did. But you know how Brigand is—talk, talk, talk, and half the time I try to tune him out. Anyway, Thebos is so old there's not a chance Brigand can make it happen, not a chance he can bring another spacecraft here."

"Chance! I don't want to hear any more about chance," Corgan cried. "Chance and coincidence—I want some good hard science and mathematics and engineering to get these Demi puppies cloned, and then I plan to fly the *Prometheus* back to Florida and beat the crap out of Brigand once and for all."

"Hey, give it a rest, Corgan. There's no reason for hostility between you and me."

Corgan blurted out, "Yes, there is! Don't you keep me out of the loop ever again! I want to know what's happening. I'm the commander of the *Prometheus*."

"Yeah, Corgan, you talk a good game."

Standing stock-still, Corgan asked coldly, "What does that mean?"

"Nothing. Let's play Go-Ball or something. You'll beat Royal and me because that's what you were made for—to win at games."

"Made to win! Yeah! I think I'm starting to figure where you're coming from." They stared at each other, neither of them moving until Corgan said, "What you mean is that I didn't win the Virtual War. Right? Is that what you mean? That I actually lost the war, but Sharla saved me by cheating? That's why Ananda was trained to fight a new war. And everybody knows it by now. Brigand has probably announced to the whole world that Corgan, who was supposed to be a hero, is nothing but a fraud!"

"Slow down! Take it easy," Cyborg said. "Nobody knows that except us. Brigand didn't tell anybody."

"He didn't?" That was a surprise.

"He'll never tell. Brigand wants people to think you're a reasonably good fighter because that makes him look all the stronger, since he's already chased you out of two domed cities. If everyone thought you were a loser, it wouldn't be much of a victory for Brigand, so he doesn't want people to think—"

"That I'm a *loser*?"

"Wait! No. I didn't say that right. I mean . . . I don't know what I mean."

Corgan stood stiffly, his jaw and his fists clenched. Was that what everyone thought of him—that he was "reasonably good" but ran away from a real battle? A loser who could fight with virtual images but who couldn't stand up to actual flesh-and-blood combat with a live tyrant?

"Hey, Corgan, don't obsess over—," Cyborg began, placing his hand on Corgan's shoulder.

"Stop touching me with that hand or I'll scorch your circuitry," Corgan growled.

"*What?* What the devil's wrong with you?" Cyborg demanded, stepping backward, glaring at him.

"Yeah, the devil. You got it. The devil's what's wrong with me. And the devil's name is Brigand."

Cyborg said quietly, "I know how much you hate him, but Brigand saved my life, Corgan."

"But that was *my* job," Corgan yelled. "*I* should have saved your life. I was in charge of you. If only Brigand had told me where you were trapped, I could have freed you."

"Brigand said time was running out, Corgan. I was drowning."

"Time! Nobody knows more about time than I do. No, he just wanted to be the dominant clone—the *hero*. But it was my fault because I should have . . . should have . . ." Corgan slumped and turned away, saying, "Never mind. Tell everyone I'm out of here for a few days." As he walked past the table where the six of them had breakfasted only an hour earlier, he reached for the machete he'd left on the bench. That cursed machete!

Thirteen

The clean sand, the clear sky, the caressing beach, the foam-capped waves rushing onto the shore, these had been Corgan's idea of paradise—once. But paradise was no longer rewarding or even bearable, not on this day. He ran into the dark, somber, dripping jungle until he could no longer run because roots and vines and branches tripped him. The farther he went, the darker the jungle became, matching his mood.

The jungle had grown so thick since he was there more than four months earlier that a trail was no longer visible. It didn't matter—Corgan knew where he was heading. Moving more slowly, he sidestepped obstacles instead of slicing the thick vines and roots. Soon he heard it: A waterfall always announced its presence before it became visible. He broke through to the clearing and there it was: the high, narrow veil of white water splashing from black volcanic rock forty meters above his head. Once, he'd thought it beautiful; now it seemed sinister. This was where the misfortune had happened.

Holding the machete flat on both his outstretched hands, as if making an offering, he lowered it to the side of the pool at the precise spot where he'd left it on that terrible day. He wished a rockslide would crash down and bury it.

He wanted to be alone, at least for a while, away from Cyborg and Delphine and Sharla, his supposed friends who'd kept pulling against him, arguing with him, accusing him. For hours he sat unmoving on a boulder at the side of the pool, trying to purge his mind and think of nothing, of no one. But disturbing thoughts kept rolling around inside his head, and he couldn't scour them away.

Would anyone miss him if he stayed here until he got his issues sorted out? Back at the lab Delphine and Sharla would be planning the Demi cloning, yet they could manage without him. He had one talent that might have helped them a bit, his time-splitting ability, but it wasn't crucial to the experiment. As the sun slid down toward the tops of the trees, Ananda and Cyborg were probably sitting together on the sand, touching. Royal would be fishing or cooking or building something for Delphine. Only Corgan was alone.

And this was a perfect place to be alone. Fish swam in the pool—lots of fish. Fruit fell to the ground and grew into more trees that bore even more fruit. Better not wish for a rockslide to bury the machete, though—if he stayed here long, he'd need the machete to gut the fish and shoot sparks from stones to light fires.

Night fell. Hours passed. The sun rose on another day. No one came to look for him. He ate, swam, caught fish, and brooded for one more night, going over all the things that had happened in the past month, the past year, trying to mentally document his slide from hero to zero. Another day and night went by, and then, unexpectedly, on the third day Sharla appeared, picking her way through the growth.

"Why are you doing this?" she asked. Not *Hello* or *We're worried about you* or *We miss you.*

"You noticed that I was gone?"

She sat beside him, curling her legs beneath her. "Feeling a little sorry for ourselves, are we?"

"It's not just that I'm feeling sorry for myself. It's more than that."

"Want to talk?" she asked. "If you do, I'm here."

He hadn't expected sympathy or caring, and he couldn't think how to answer. His mood lightened just a bit. Sharla waited for him to speak, and when he didn't, she said, "Delphine implanted four blastocysts into the dog. She's hoping at least one of them will develop."

"How long before she knows?" he asked.

"A week, maybe less. She's an amazing woman, Corgan. I learned a lot from her, and not just about implantation. She's had a lot of rough spots in her life, but she just kept picking up the pieces and moving on. More than anything she wanted a baby of her own. Radiation poisoning in a nuclear accident not only left her sterile, it caused a tumor that had to be removed, so she couldn't even be implanted with someone else's child. I guess that's why she keeps trying to mother all of us. And she has a lot of wisdom to pass along."

"So does Thebos," Corgan answered.

Ignoring that, Sharla continued, "It would make Delphine ecstatically happy if we all stayed here forever on Nuku Hiva."

Corgan shook his head. "This whole island is haunted by bad memories. Don't you feel it?"

Sharla scoffed, "No, I don't feel it, and neither does anyone else. It's you who's haunted, Corgan. I mean, what made you come right here, to this particular pool where Cyborg lost his hand?" She glanced at the pool, glanced back at him.

"Because I know this is where the really bad stuff in my life first began," he answered. "With my big mistake. You heard what Delphine said—'if by chance Corgan hadn't left the machete at the side of the pool'—"

Sharla interrupted with, "Wrong! You misinterpreted because you never let Delphine finish. She was actually going to say that if you hadn't, by chance, left the machete where you did, Cyborg might have drowned. Meaning it was a lucky thing, a good thing, that you dropped it where Brigand could find it."

"That's what she really meant?"

"Yes! And she was right. Think about it!" More quietly Sharla said, "I was here, Corgan, remember? I saw it all. Brigand cut Cyborg loose from the boulder, but that was only the first part. It's you, Corgan, who saved Cyborg's life. You're the one who forced the water out of his lungs, you're the one who ran, carrying him in your arms, all the way back to the lab, where Delphine kept him from bleeding to death. You were his savior."

Savior. How could she call him a savior? "He was my responsibility, and I failed him."

"Wrong again!" After a breath Sharla went on, "You obsess over Cyborg's lost hand way more than he does. As if it were a colossal mistake you made. You need to reevaluate, Corgan. You've got to see that you played the part of the hero in that rescue."

His spirits began to rise. She'd almost persuaded him, and she might have if she'd stopped right there, but then she had to add, "And you've done a lot of other really great things too. Like, you won the Virtual War!"

His sense of redemption sank as if shot by an arrow. Climbing to his feet, he cried, "You know that's not true, Sharla. Back in the Wyoming DC, right before Brigand's revolt, you admitted that you cheated in the Virtual War to make it look like I won. I didn't want that to happen," he insisted, pounding his thigh with a fist. "Before I met you, I never did anything wrong in my whole life. Then after we met, you broke the code and got me out of my virtual Box, and I lied about that to Mendor, and that's when everything started to go wrong, and after that things just kept getting worse."

"So it's all my fault?" she asked hotly. "Everything is?"

He sank back onto the ground and told her, "No, it's not your fault. I wanted those things to happen. I wanted to be free and to be with you. I liked being a hero, only I wasn't a real hero."

"And that's what you want to be. A real hero."

"Right. A real one. Not a fake."

"Then, start with this," she said, coming close to him. "Listen to what I'm saying. Back in the Wyo-DC you were rushing to escape from Brigand's rebels, and I didn't have time to tell you the whole truth about the war. You heard only about the cheating. There's more to the story."

Corgan waited, holding his breath, half afraid of what was coming.

"When we were fighting the Virtual War," Sharla continued, "the two other federation teams broke a lot of rules. I saw what they were doing, but I kept ahead of them— mostly." With vehemence she added, "If they'd played honestly, by the rules, you would have won, hands down. When it came close to the end, the guys from the Eurasian Alliance pulled a quick fake maneuver that I didn't catch in time, so I recoded the clock. I added a hundredth of a second. That's how you won—we said they didn't get their troops to the top of the hill at exactly the right split second."

Corgan couldn't believe it. He gasped, "You mean *every-body* cheated?"

"A whole lot more than I did." She nodded, looking directly at him. "I swear on my life that what I just told you is the truth. So you're going to ask me why I didn't report what happened. I didn't because there'd have been a big blowup and a rematch right away, and poor little Brig just couldn't take that. He was half dead by the time the war was over. I had to protect him."

Sharla moved even closer, and this time she reached out to Corgan. With her hand on his cheek she said, "And you . . . you told me before the war that you wanted so much to come here to Nuku Hiva—what good would it have done if I'd started all that trouble? The more I analyzed it, the more I believed that if the war had been totally honest, you'd have won big-time. And I blamed myself—if I'd been smarter and faster, I could have knocked those other punks right on their butts. But mostly, what I did was because of Brig."

"Wow!" Corgan moved to sit with his back against the tree, and Sharla slid down beside him, her shoulder next to his. Her hair smelled good, like the frangipani blossoms. He tried to absorb not just the scent of her, but all that she'd told him. Did it change things? Yes. It brought him up one rung on the hero ladder, but he still had a lot of rungs to climb.

"I've been doing some thinking these past few days," he

told her. "About good choices getting screwed up by bad chance, like Delphine said. It's what keeps happening to me."

"Welcome to the world, Corgan. That's what life is like. Real life, not virtual reality." Leaning closer, she said, "But you have so much to be proud of. You left Demi on the station to save both me from brain damage and Cyborg from premature aging and death—so that means you've saved Cyborg's life twice. And you really did win the war. Corgan, I believe in you. You're good, you're strong, you're decent. Why don't you believe in yourself?"

Humbly he answered, "I'm working on it. I just can't seem to get it all together. What makes you so wise, Sharla? We were both born in the same lab on the same day."

Her smile looked a little off center, tinged with irony. "Because I was a naughty kid and I broke out of my virtual-reality Box when I was seven. I met real people, in secret, and I saw them labor and sweat and die. You stayed protected in your own little Box till two years ago. For all those years you were clueless, and you're still clueless a lot. But that's just you, Corgan."

"No, it isn't. Not for long," he promised her. "I'm ready to take charge. I know what I need to do."

Maybe she believed him, maybe not. When he asked, "Will you stay here tonight?" she began, "I really should go back to the lab and check on . . . ," but after his arm tightened around her, she decided, speaking slowly, "I guess Delphine doesn't really need me. Yes, I'll stay."

Later, as the stars brightened, Corgan knew what he was *not* going to do. Sharla might have let him, but this wasn't the right time. Too many elements of their lives remained unresolved.

Were her feelings for him friendly, romantic, or just tolerant? And how did he feel about her? He loved her and he always had, but it was an insecure love without enough trust. He suspected she might fly straight into Brigand's arms as soon as she saw him again.

And then there was the age thing. So complicated! Sharla was now sixteen for eternity. Brigand kept aging two years every month, which should make him about twenty-two right now; twenty-two and counting. Corgan was sixteen but would mature normally, eventually reaching middle age and beyond while Sharla stayed at sixteen. Maybe he ought to forget all those mathematics and just love her in this moment, here, now, in the warmth of the night. Love her with his heart and arms and mouth . . . and that's all, he decided. He wouldn't attempt anything more than that.

Sharla slept, but Corgan stayed alert, planning his next moves. The night was long and lonely, even though she lay there beside the pool with her head on his lap, her golden hair spread across her cheek. At dawn, when she awoke, her blue eyes reflecting the perfect sky, Corgan said reluctantly, "We need to go back."

"To Florida? I can't talk you out of it?"

"No."

"It scares me," she murmured. "I couldn't bear it if I lost you."

"It's like Delphine was saying," he told her, "about choice and chance. I've chosen this duty to make sure Thebos stays safe, and I'll have to take my chances."

There was one last act he had to perform before they left this waterfall. He picked up the machete and flung it high into the air, where it arced, spun, and then fell precisely into the center of the pool, splashing as it hit. That gesture might not wash away all the bad memories, but it was a start.

As he pushed through the jungle once again, Sharla stayed behind him, stepping carefully across the gnarled roots of trees that must have been standing there before all the islanders died of plague. They arrived at the beach just as the sun cleared the horizon. "We'll stop here," Corgan said, pointing to the lab. "I'll tell Delphine first."

They found her peering into the cage where the dog, Diva, lay. "She's getting tamer," Delphine said before she even said hello. "She seems to know we don't want to hurt her. Last night she ate out of my hand." Smiling as she turned toward them, she asked, "And where were you two last night?"

"In the middle of a long conversation," Sharla answered. "And now Corgan has some news for you."

After he told her, Delphine reacted the way Sharla had predicted: Her eyes swam with tears and she cried, "But we've been so happy here, all of us, all together! Do you really have to go, Corgan? Sharla and Cyborg and Ananda, too?"

"That'll be up to them," he answered. "But you and Royal can come with us if you want to. There's room. . . ."

Even before he'd finished, Delphine started to shake her head. "Royal loves it here. He says that Nuku Hiva is the home he was destined for. He feels it's part of his heritage."

This was no surprise—Corgan had figured as much. All night long he'd tried to think about what would be best for all of them, especially Delphine, and he'd come up with a possibility that he was now ready to offer. "I owe you, Delphine," he began. "For a lot of things. And I have this idea—uh, maybe you ought to sit down."

"Goodness!" She laughed a little, without mirth. "That sounds mysterious." But she moved to the chair Royal had built for her; it looked something like a throne.

Corgan pulled up a stool in front of her and leaned forward to look into her eyes. "What would you think about being Lockered, Delphine?"

"You mean, be young again?" Her eyes widened as her hands clutched each other.

"Any age you want," he told her. "You can be the same age as Royal, and I can Locker Royal so he won't ever get any older, just like Sharla and Cyborg are frozen at the ages they are now. You just figure out the date you want to go back to, and you get inside and I turn on the power and—"

"That would be incredible!" Delphine breathed. "Unbelievable! But I don't know . . . what if I . . . ? You mean, any age at all?"

Sharla nodded but warned, "It gets really complicated. It stops your life at a certain age and you stay there forever. There are things I'm still not sure about, like will I keep learning more and more and start to think like a mature person, or will I always think like a sixteen-year-old?"

"Yes, that's pretty scary," Delphine agreed, but then she grabbed Sharla's arm and apologized, "You're extremely mature for a sixteen-year-old, Sharla. It's just . . . yes, I'd like to be Lockered, and I'm really grateful that you'd let me, Corgan, but I'll have to do an awful lot of thinking before I can decide what age I want to be permanently. How long do I have before I make my decision?"

"By tomorrow," Corgan answered. "I want to leave here tomorrow."

Delphine gasped, "So soon! And so much to think about! What about Diva? What about the dog? I don't even know yet if the implanted embryos will mature."

"I don't see that it's a real problem," Sharla assured her. "Diva's either going to be pregnant or she isn't. You can teach me how to take care of her when she goes with us. If she's going to bear a Demi clone, she needs to be where Ananda is, and I'm pretty sure Ananda'll want to go back to Florida. Corgan told me Ananda is treated like a princess in the Flor-DC."

"Yeah, Ananda's their hero," Corgan agreed. "Okay, I've got a lot to do, so I need to start." On his way through the door he called back, "You and Royal think about it, Delphine, and tell me what you decide by tomorrow morning. Come on, Sharla. Let's go talk to Ananda and Cyborg."

Fourteen

The reaction was not what Corgan had expected. While Ananda looked unsure, Cyborg said he wanted to stay on Nuku Hiva.

"And not go back to Florida?" Corgan asked him, astonished.

"I don't mean exactly that . . . it's more like I don't want *you* to go back," Cyborg answered. "Not if it turns into a death match between you and Brigand."

Corgan swung his leg across a fallen tree trunk and sat there as he demanded, "Which is it, Cyborg? You're afraid *I'm* going to die or you're afraid *he's* going to die?"

"Corgan, I don't want anybody to die. If you say we have to go back, let me try to negotiate a peace between you and Brigand. I'm a strategist, remember?"

"Yeah, I remember. And I remember that Brigand is also a strategist. You can negotiate as much as you want—his strategy will be to agree to anything you say. Then he'll probably stab me in the back, but I have to take my chances. Because of Thebos."

Trying to remain reasonable, Cyborg said, "You need to consider all the possibilities. What Brigand channeled to me about forcing Thebos to build another *Prometheus* and then fly it here—that could be a big lie."

"I understand that," Corgan said. "But I just can't take a chance, because it might be true, which means I have to protect Thebos. So I need to hear from both you and Ananda, are you coming with me tomorrow?"

"The answer should be obvious," Cyborg told him. "Haven't I always been with you? Leaving the Wyo-DC, leaving the Flor-DC, I was your man then and I'm your man now."

"And where Cyborg goes, I go," Ananda added. "We're with you."

"Great! There's still one more person I'd better go and tell. Well, not really a person. I have to talk to Mendor."

As Corgan hurried up the hill, his mind was full of details that needed attending to in order to prepare for tomorrow's flight. Inside the barn, when he pushed open the LiteSuit material that marked off the makeshift Box, he heard a voice that was neither male nor female say, "I could sense your agitation the second you appeared. Tell me what's happening, Corgan. Do you need my help?"

"I don't think so, Mendor. It's just that I have a lot to do. We're leaving here tomorrow. I have to go back to Florida and deal with Brigand."

Was it illusion, or did Mendor's green eyes grow larger, rounder, becoming more appealing, like a baby's? "Take me with you," Mendor said softly.

"Huh?"

"I can assist you. I can provide useful information. I wouldn't be difficult to transport, Corgan—you can compress me into a package no bigger than the palm of your hand."

This was unexpected. "Why would you want to come with me?"

"Because when you're not here, I die. After little Cyborg left, I was programmed to work only with you, Corgan." The voice, usually so placid, rose in intensity. "When you're with me, I come alive. Now you may be about to battle for your life. Let me help you to defeat Brigand. I know I can help."

Why not? Corgan shrugged. "Sure, Mendor. I'll ask Sharla to pack you. She'll know how to disconnect and compress you."

Spherical waves of pleasure seemed to radiate out of Mendor's image as the face changed from gold to warm flesh tones. "Thank you," he/she breathed. "I won't fail you."

Corgan left Mendor and stepped into the darkened barn. He saw his blue LiteSuit lying across the bunk, clean and unwrinkled, and wondered who'd laundered it—Sharla? Not likely. Delphine? Probably. Whoever had done it, he was grateful, because as the commander of the *Prometheus*, he needed to look good. Still, he would hate to say good-bye to his old jeans.

Hurrying down the hill, he called loudly, "Sharla, do you hear me?"

A flash of sunlight on golden hair moving through the trees showed that she'd heard and she was heading toward him. "Is something wrong?" she cried when she was still eight meters away. "What do you need?"

"You. I need you." As they came together, he grasped her hands and asked, "Would you please give me a haircut?"

"A haircut?" This time when she laughed at him, he didn't mind. It felt good to hear her laughter, strong and full and genuine. "I guess I can manage that."

He sat on a log while she began combing and snipping his hair with scissors she borrowed from Delphine. "You have great hair," she told him. "On top of your head, I mean. I'm not such a big fan of your facial hair. You need a shave."

"Right." He didn't have a razor, but he knew Royal had one. Although Royal was younger than Corgan, he had a pretty thick line of black hairs on his upper lip, probably even more than on Corgan's, but hey—it wasn't a contest. "Don't stop," he pleaded when Sharla put down the scissors.

"But it'll get too short," she told him. "Your hair looks fine now."

"Thanks, but—could you keep combing for a while longer?" Her fingers in his hair soothed him, let him relax enough that he'd be able to deal with leaving this island, which had once again begun to feel like paradise. Maybe Sharla was right—the haunted feelings had all been inside Corgan.

Sharla mentioned, "Delphine wants to make a farewell dinner for us tonight and then have one more dance around the fire. She says nothing will ever be as good again as this time we've had together. She wants tonight, our last night, to be special."

"I can deal with that. I'll even dance, if you promise to wear that dress again."

That evening, as the sun drew closer to the horizon, Corgan and Sharla walked down the hill together. He still had on his jeans, and Sharla, as she'd promised, wore her tapa cloth dress for this one last time on Nuku Hiva, and maybe the last time ever. Delphine stood in front of the table, her arms outstretched to welcome them. Cyborg and Ananda were already seated; Royal came forward from the barbecue pit bearing a wooden tray with a steaming rib roast of beef and two huge lobsters. As he set it on the table, Delphine said, "Raise your glasses, everyone."

They weren't really glasses, just laboratory beakers full of mango juice, but everyone did as she asked. "Here's to the finest young people on the face of the earth," Delphine toasted them. "To Corgan, may you find success. To Sharla, who will forever be a beautiful sixteen-year-old. To Ananda, who will have two new copies of her beloved Demi—yes, I confirmed that today; they're growing. To Cyborg, destined to advise Earth's rulers with his wise and decent judgments. And . . ." Delphine's voice grew softer, "To Royal, a prince in every way."

Corgan wondered if he was supposed to say something in response, but Cyborg spoke first. "To Delphine, whose brilliant mind is matched only by her boundless heart."

That did it for Delphine; she couldn't hold back the tears any longer. Ananda and Sharla hurried to comfort her, one on each side, their arms around her, their hair—Sharla's pale gold and Ananda's ebony—sweeping across Delphine's face as they bent over her. The three males—Royal, Corgan, and Cyborg—sat there awkwardly, not knowing what to do when a grown woman cried.

It wasn't until after they'd eaten their feast, as the last edge of the visible sun gleamed like a ruby on the crown of the waves, not until they'd built their fire—bigger than usual—and danced around it, sweating from the movement and the heat, that Corgan sought to win the most important commitment.

He took Sharla's hand and led her into the trees as the music still drummed in the background. The heat of the night and the jungle's dampness made the scent of flowers almost dizzying. Putting his arms around her, he asked, "Sharla, will you be coming with me tomorrow?"

"I will. Because I want to be there for you. You saved me when I needed you most. You risked everything to take me to the space station, and the Locker fixed me. I'll never desert you, Corgan."

Joy filled him, and he wanted to stay and savor the moment, but there was one more thing he needed to do. "Let's go," he told her.

"Where?"

"To the *Prometheus*. If we're Lockering Delphine tomorrow morning, I want to be sure everything's working right. I haven't checked inside the *Prometheus* since we got home from the dog hunt."

Ananda and Cyborg had disappeared somewhere together. Tiptoeing past Delphine and Royal, Corgan overheard enough fragments of conversation to know they were talking about Lockering. "Wait, I want to take off my shoes," Sharla said, pulling back. "This might be my last chance to walk in the sand. I'll probably never get to come back here again."

Corgan took off his shoes too, and the two of them ran into the edges of the waves and then back to the beach. Sand stuck to their wet feet and wedged between their toes. Each time they went into the waves to wash off the sand, it covered them again on the beach, making them laugh like two little kids. "Maybe we shouldn't leave," Sharla said. "Maybe we should stay here forever."

"Maybe we *can* come back one day," Corgan told her. "Once I take care of what needs to be done, I'll be free. If I'm still alive."

"Don't say that!"

They reached the *Prometheus*. Though there was no moon, enough light came from the stars to let Corgan again admire the craft, a sphere flattened both top and bottom. He offered his cupped hands to support Sharla's foot to give her a boost up the side so she could reach the entrance. To minimize air friction, Thebos had installed only one handhold, near the top. After Sharla opened the hatch and slid down into the *Prometheus*, Corgan followed her.

Sharla mentioned, "We brought sand in on our feet. Is that a problem?"

"I'll sweep it up tomorrow before we launch," he told her.

He touched the control panel, lighting it. He didn't need to turn on the power to read that the fuel cells were full—more than a week's worth of sunlight streaming onto the solar panels had recharged everything. "I installed these monitors myself," he told Sharla. "Thebos told me how to do it. You don't remember anything about Thebos, do you?"

"No." She frowned. "I don't remember anything that happened between crashing through the dome and then climbing out of the Locker in the space station, when I'd become sixteen forever. I keep thinking about Delphine. Do you wonder what age she'll choose?"

"Not really, but I am thinking about age. Someone else's. Before Cyborg got Lockered, Brigand kept channeling pain into Cyborg's head and blitzing him with psychic commands to come back to Florida. Then, after the Lockering, all that stopped. Cyborg said he could tell that Brigand was happy for him."

In the darkness they couldn't see each other too well, but Corgan sensed that Sharla knew exactly where he was going with this. He said, "Could that charge from the Locker have reached all the way through Cyborg and entered Brigand, ten thousand kilometers away? And if that happened, is Brigand now permanently sixteen just like Cyborg, and neither of them will die of premature aging?"

"Corgan, I don't have a clue. I don't know whether something like that is even possible," Sharla told him. "I created both of them, but I still haven't figured out how that psychic connection works. Brigand's a lot better at it than Cyborg. He controls it, turning it on and off when he doesn't want Cyborg to know something."

"So Cyborg isn't sure whether Brigand got Lockered by remote channeling? Or did you even ask him."

"No. I mean yes, I asked him, but he doesn't know. We won't find out till we're back in the Flor-DC."

Would it make any difference? Corgan wondered. If they got into a battle, would age play a part? It probably would. If Brigand was now six years older than Corgan, he'd be bigger, stronger, faster. And maybe . . . smarter.

Corgan shivered, and not because the *Prometheus* felt cooler than the weather outside.

Fifteen

Corgan couldn't sleep. All night long his brain throbbed with plans, tactics, calculations, and lists of essentials. Before the first glow of dawn he rolled off the bunk and went to a nearby stream, where he knelt naked in the cold water, washing every centimeter of himself. Then he took Royal's razor from the shelf in the barn; without asking permission, he used it to shave his face clean. Last, he pulled on his LiteSuit and picked up Mendor—Sharla had compacted the program the night before.

The sun had barely risen as he strode down the hill, but he figured everyone would be awake on this important day. He was right; Delphine had food ready and insisted that all of them eat. As they sat around the table—for the last time—Corgan asked her, "Have you decided, Delphine?"

She folded her napkin, creasing it carefully. "Yes. But you can ask Royal first."

Royal sat on the edge of the bench, hunched over with his hands dangling between his knees. "I don't want to be Lockered," he said, his voice low. "I want to grow up to be a man. Like my father. And then I want to be an old man. Like my grandfather." Royal looked from one to the other and explained, "And I want to stay on Nuku Hiva. I could never live under a dome, because I love the sea and the rain forest too much."

"Did your grandfather tell you that's what you're supposed to do?" Ananda wondered.

"No. It's my own decision," he assured her. "But Ananda, remember what my grandfather said on Hiva Oa? He told me that everything will be tranquil when two Royals take me where my heart will lie. Well, this is where my heart lies."

In the silence that followed, one by one each of them turned expectantly toward Delphine. "My turn?" she asked. "Well, after a great deal of thought I've chosen to be Lockered. I want to become twenty-eight years old."

"Really?" Ananda came right out and asked her, "Why twenty-eight, Delphine? Is it because you want to be young and strong again? Then, why not twenty or twenty-one?"

Delphine smiled a little. "The answer to your first question is yes, I want to be young and strong again. As for the second question—why twenty-eight? Because there's such a lack of data about Lockering."

"Huh? I don't get the connection between answers one and two," Cyborg stated.

As they all looked at Delphine quizzically, she began to explain, "You see, kids, I'd received all my university degrees by the time I was twenty-four, and then I spent the next four years doing original research on genetics. I want to retain all that knowledge. If I were to go back to twenty years old, would I lose all memory of those eight years of learning and experimentation? Would they be erased? I can't tell."

She glanced from one to the other. When she saw they still didn't comprehend, she continued, "We have only two samples of Lockering that I could possibly research—Cyborg and Sharla. Cyborg has told me he remembers everything that happened between his two dates—the date of his Lockering and the date of the age he was returned to. He remembers, but Sharla doesn't recall anything between *her* two dates. Of course, Sharla was brain-damaged, so that's a mitigating factor. Anyway, a mere two cases are not a large enough sampling for any scientist to create reliable data. I'd need at least a hundred research subjects who'd been Lockered, and that number doesn't exist. So I'll return myself to age twenty-eight, to the time when I'd done most of my major work, just so I can feel certain that all that input will stay in my brain. Understand?"

"I . . . guess so," Cyborg answered. "Maybe we could discuss it more."

Because the clock in his head kept ticking toward the departure time, Corgan said, "Not now. We need to get moving. Sharla, you take Delphine to the *Prometheus*. The rest of you can wait here. We won't be long."

Corgan hurried toward the spaceship to arrive ahead of Sharla and Delphine. He leaped up and grabbed the handhold, then opened the hatch to swing himself through it. There was now enough daylight inside to illuminate the whole deck. Quickly he swept the sand from the night before into an empty metal box and climbed through the hatch to throw the sand over the side. Holding the box, he jumped to the ground just as Delphine and Sharla reached him.

"Sharla first," he said. He felt a bit disappointed because instead of a dress Sharla was again wearing the LiteSuit, the gold-colored one she'd borrowed from Corgan. Since it was too large, she'd cinched the waist with a strip of tapa cloth. After Sharla had entered the ship, Corgan said, "Now you,

Delphine," but even standing on the box Delphine couldn't stretch quite high enough. With a lot of pushing by Corgan and pulling by Sharla they got her inside the *Prometheus*.

Immediately Corgan turned on the power to the Locker, listening closely as the motor started up. It sounded right, and when he laid his hands on the outside to feel the vibrations, they seemed to be throbbing at the correct microspeed. Next he opened the Locker and asked Delphine, "Want to take a look inside? This is your last chance to change your mind. After you enter, you'll be strapped in and I'll close the door. You don't have claustrophobia or anything, do you?"

"No, I'm fine." Still, she appeared a little apprehensive about the makeshift construction of the Locker. Taking a deep breath, she told him, "The date I'd like to return to is September 20, 2060. Can you do that, Corgan?"

"Any special reason for that date, Delphine?" Sharla asked her.

"It's right before I began my relationship with Grimber. I'm actually hoping Lockering will erase *that* part of my memory."

Since Corgan remembered what a disagreeable man Grimber had been, he could totally sympathize with Delphine's choice. But maybe memory erasing wouldn't happen. As Delphine had said, they had no real data. "Okay, I'm setting the dials now," he said. "Sharla, help her into the Locker. Is she going to fit?"

"She fits fine. This is exactly how they did it with me, Delphine," Sharla commented as she settled a thin metal helmet onto Delphine's head. "These metal cuffs go around your arms. It might seem kind of scary, but—"

"I'm not scared. I'm excited. I can't wait for it to start."

Sharla closed the door, Corgan threw the switch, and the whine of machinery built up to a crescendo. He stared intently at the whirring dials as they spun backward by minutes, hours, days, years, all the way to 2060—December, November, October. . . . At September 20 he smacked the red button that stopped the power, and the whine of the motor wound down to a low buzz, then died.

"I'll open it," Sharla said, glancing at Corgan. Both of them knew this was the moment for worry. If anything had gone wrong, they were about to find out.

Sharla unsealed the door and out stepped Delphine. Becoming young hadn't turned her into a raving beauty, but her flesh was firm and she was a lot thinner—the tapa cloth dress hung on her in folds. Her lips were full, her hair was as wild as ever but without any gray, and her eyes shone with joy. "How do I look?" she asked.

"You look wonderful!" Sharla exclaimed.

This time Delphine had no problem sliding down from the hatch of the *Prometheus*; she even jumped the last meter and landed firmly on her feet. "I feel so young! I *am* young!" she cried, almost singing it as she headed back toward the lab. "Does anyone have a mirror?"

Standing in the shadow of the trees, half hidden, Royal was waiting. He must have liked the way Delphine turned out, because when he saw her, he stepped forward quickly, smiling and saying, "Greetings, Miss Delphine. I'm here to escort you back to the lab. I thought you might feel a little shaky after being Lockered."

"I feel great!" she exclaimed. "But thanks for coming. I'll

race you back." Delphine started to run, with Royal sprinting after her to catch up.

"Hey, Royal," Corgan shouted after them. "Tell Cyborg and Ananda to come here right now. We need to get everything control-tested so we can take off. We're losing time."

When they arrived, the four of them loaded their gear first, stowing it so it wouldn't float around when the *Prometheus* shed gravity. Then Cyborg brought water to fill the containers. Sharla found a safe place to secure Mendor— she'd condensed the program to its smallest size. Ananda secured Diva's cage to the inside deck so the dog wouldn't float around in zero gravity, and she murmured softly to Diva, trying to calm her. "This must be so frightening for her," she said. "But I think she's bonding to me. She's been licking my hand when I feed her."

Or maybe it was Ananda who was bonding to Diva. In spite of all the protests she'd made that no dog would ever be able to take Demi's place, she was paying a lot of attention to this wild yellow dog who whimpered for Ananda to pick her up and hold her.

Corgan supervised the inspection of every instrument in the *Prometheus*, making sure nothing essential to flight could be overlooked. He issued orders and the others obeyed, knowing that only Corgan understood the operations of the spaceship. By the time the sun reached its zenith, they were ready to take off. Outside, Delphine and Royal stood on the concrete pad, waiting to watch the launch. While Corgan adjusted the touch-screen monitors, his three passengers grinned with anticipation because they knew what would happen when the *Prometheus* took off.

"Here we go," Corgan said, but Cyborg yelled, "Wait! Stop! Something's happening!"

Through the port they could see Royal take a running leap up the side of the *Prometheus*. He must have grabbed the outside handle to hold on, because he started pounding on the hatch.

"He's changed his mind and wants to go with us!" Ananda cried. "Quick, open the hatch."

While the pounding continued, Corgan quickly turned off the spacecraft's thrusters, then touched the button that unlocked the hatch. Cyborg yanked it open, shouting, "Get inside," as he reached for Royal.

"No, I'm fine, I'm not coming in," Royal answered. He held on to the edge, resting his shoulders and arms on the inner ledge of the hatch. Visible only from the chest up while the rest of him hung outside the spacecraft, he said, "I need to tell Corgan something."

Corgan, startled, asked him, "What?"

Royal spoke as casually as if they were having a conversation at the picnic table. "My grandfather gave me a message in a dream. It was for you, Corgan."

"Me?"

"Yes. He came to me in the dream the first night you went out there in the jungle by yourself, and then after you got back, I kind of forgot about it. I'm glad I remembered before you left here."

"What . . . uh, what did your grandfather say?" Corgan asked him.

"He said, 'Tell this to Corgan: If you don't lose your head, you'll win.'"

141

Taken aback, Corgan repeated, "If I don't lose my head, I'll win?"

"You got it," Royal said, nodding as if the message weren't particularly astonishing.

"Did you ask him to explain that?" Corgan wanted to know, but this time Royal answered with a head shake.

"I don't talk in these dreams, I just listen to my grandfather. So that's it. At least I got to tell you before you left. Have a safe trip." And with that Royal let go and slid down the hull to the ground, where Delphine waited.

"Weird!" Ananda breathed.

"Really weird," Sharla agreed. "But . . . is it supposed to be a warning?"

"I can't worry about it now," Corgan answered, although he was more than a little perplexed. "Lock the hatch, Cyborg. Everybody hold on to something. We're taking off."

The *Prometheus* slowly lifted itself from the ground while Sharla and Ananda waved wildly at Delphine and Royal beneath them. Each girl gripped a bar with one hand and waved with the other, but when weightlessness hit, their bodies rose horizontally behind them as though they were stretched out facedown on an invisible bed. Kicking her feet in empty air, Ananda cried, "I *love* antigravity propulsion! Let's dance, Cyborg."

Cyborg, usually so serious, fell under the spell of weightlessness too and turned somersaults in the air, looping around Ananda, laughing and reaching out to give her little pinches as she squealed and tried to grab him. Sharla sailed to Corgan and spun around him until they bumped into Ananda and Cyborg, sending all four of them flying in different directions.

It was fun, but, "I gotta watch what I'm doing," Corgan said. He needed to confirm that their ascent over Nuku Hiva was vertically accurate.

From six hundred meters high the lush green growth, blue waters, and white-capped waves sent a pang of regret through Corgan because he was once again leaving this Eden. At two kilometers the shape of the mountain ridges revealed how volcanoes had created the island and how erosion had sculpted the valleys. At four kilometers the whole island was visible, with fringes of land reaching out into the sea like tentacles, and by eight Corgan began to see the entire chain of the Isles of Hiva.

No more time for sightseeing, and no more time to play games in weightlessness. "Sit down and strap in," he told them. "I'm ready to generate the gravitational field."

With a thud, gravity returned and their bodies felt normal again. Corgan set the course for east-northeast at an altitude of eight kilometers. Until they got close to Florida, he wouldn't need to pay much attention to navigation. But other matters required a lot of attention.

"Cyborg," he began, "I'm going to need your cooperation."

"I thought I'd already been cooperating," he answered. "What else?"

"I can't let you know where I plan to land. If I do, Brigand will siphon the information out of your brain and he'll be waiting with his New Rebel Troops when we get there. He already knows we're on our way, I guess."

Cyborg nodded apologetically. "I guess. I'm sorry. I can't help it."

"I know you can't. So I'm asking you to stay separated from the rest of us. Go down into the galley. Go into one of the closets so you won't hear anything we say here on the deck, and stay there. When we get close to where we'll land, I'll come and get you. Then I'll have to blindfold you."

Frowning, Cyborg clenched and unclenched his real hand for a long minute, then answered, "I understand the logic. I'll do what you say."

"Cyborg . . ." Ananda reached out to him.

"It's okay," he said. "See you all later. Somewhere."

"That's kind of cruel," Ananda murmured after he'd gone. "But he's being great about it, isn't he? So, where are we going to land?"

"Come over here," Corgan told Ananda and Sharla, "and I'll show you." He touched the monitor screen to create a three-dimensional hologram of Earth. "Wait, let me ratchet it up," he said, making the hologram loom larger and spin slowly. "Here's where we are," pointing to the central Pacific. "Here's where we're going." He showed them Florida. "We're traveling pretty slow because flying through Earth's atmosphere takes longer than flying above it in Earth orbit like we did before. But slow is good because I want it to be dark when we get there. There's no moon tonight."

As he turned from the hologram, Corgan explained, "When we left the Flor-DC, we flew up through the hole in the dome that Brigand smashed when he crashed the Harrier, which you don't remember, Sharla, because you were brain-injured then. Well, we can't get back into the city the same way we flew out, because the dome has been fixed. Cyborg told me that—he got it from Brigand, and I believe it because they were working on the dome when we left. With the hole sealed up again, there's no entrance."

"Then, how will you . . . ," Ananda began.

During those restless hours of the long, sleepless night Corgan had worked it all out. "We'll have to land without any light at all," he told them. "Even a small or dim light would be visible from the Flor-DC, and Brigand's going to be watching for us. Ananda, I'll need your sharp eyes to help me see in the dark. Sharla, I'll need your sharp mind to calculate the distances I give you down to single meters. It doesn't matter that you can't remember Florida, Sharla, because even Ananda doesn't know exactly where we're going to land. Only I do."

"Tell us!" Ananda urged.

Looking down through the port in front of him, Corgan saw islands beneath them. He checked the hologram of the slowly rotating Earth and saw that the islands were named Hawaii. They were on course. It would be a while before they reached darkness, before they reached their destination, enough time to rehearse his plan thoroughly, to go over every detail with Sharla and Ananda.

"We'll be landing inside a bomb crater," he told them.

Sixteen

Time was one thing the devastation hadn't altered. Even though Earth was mostly destroyed on its surface, it still rotated at the same pace; it still orbited the sun.

"There's six hours' time difference between Florida and where we are now," Corgan told them. "I don't want to get to Florida until dark, so we're gonna take a detour and fly low over the Wyo-DC and do reconnaissance. Mendor can probably catch some sound waves that leak through the dome."

"If the Wyo rebels see us," Sharla objected, "they'll message Brigand through the fiber-optic cable."

"They won't see us. Look at the Earth hologram—it shows the weather all over the planet. There's plenty of cloud cover above Wyoming to hide us even if the rebels were looking for us, which they won't be. While Mendor's checking for sound waves, we can scope the dome through the infrared instruments to see if anything looks different. We'll just circle above Wyo and try to pick up information."

"Why do you want to do that?" Ananda asked.

It took him a moment to answer, "Call it long-range planning."

Sharla became alert at that. "You're making plans about the Wyo-DC?" she asked.

He stalled. "Let's say I'm trying to consider future options. If I *have* a future, if Brigand doesn't kill me as soon as we get to the Flor-DC." He gave a short laugh, but Ananda and Sharla glared at him, letting him know this was not something to joke about.

Ananda said, "Since we have extra time, I'd like to go down to the galley and wait with Cyborg. I won't say anything to him about where we'll be landing."

"Bad idea," he told her. "No way, Ananda. You might accidentally let something slip."

"I wouldn't leak anything. Trust me."

"It's not that I don't trust you, but you get carried away sometimes when you're around Cyborg, and I'd rather not take a chance."

"I said I wouldn't!" Ananda insisted, her voice escalating. "I'm a responsible human being, Corgan. Sometimes you treat me like a baby."

He half rose in his chair. "I know you wouldn't mean to spill anything, Ananda, but *do not go to Cyborg*! If you try to, I'll wrestle you to the deck. You're strong and I'm strong, and it would probably be an even match and we'd both get hammered, and then Cyborg would zap me with his bionic hand for messing with his girl, so I'd be double trashed. And where would that leave you, since I'm the only one who can fly the *Prometheus*?"

As if testing him, Ananda started to move toward the stairs, but Corgan got there first, blocking the passage.

"Oh, all right!" Ananda yielded irritably. "Although I could probably take down both you and Sharla at the same time without even half trying."

"How about just one of us? Would you like to try that?" Sharla asked, rising to the challenge. "Corgan, turn off the gravity."

Corgan hooted. "I'm staying out of this one. I want to watch the two of you duke it out in zero gravity." He touched the switch to disconnect the energized gravitational field, and in a split second weightlessness struck. Right away Ananda launched herself at Sharla but flew past her and bounced off a wall. Sharla started to giggle as Ananda swung a fist, which did nothing except propel both of them backward. With their hair unleashed by zero gravity to spread around their heads in clouds—one gold, one raven—they looked like sea goddesses battling underwater.

Sharla, always graceful, maneuvered herself across the cockpit, diving down and then floating upward, frustrating Ananda, who couldn't catch her. By then Corgan was laughing riotously as he hovered around the periphery of the deck. Quickly Ananda twisted her body to change direction and go after him. She landed a fist on top of his head, which made him bounce off the deck and rebound up through the Earth hologram, emerging at the North Pole. He dived for Ananda and caught her around the knees. Then Sharla caught Corgan around the knees, and the three of them rotated lengthwise like a lumpy sea serpent. Even Ananda laughed so hard she got the hiccups.

"We'll declare a truce," Sharla offered. "Shake hands on it."

When Ananda reached to clasp Sharla's hand, the two of them began to spin around each other faster and faster, twirling like two dolls caught in a whirlpool, squealing with glee. "It's impossible to fight in zero gravity!" Ananda shrieked. "That's why Corgan wouldn't fight me, because he knew he couldn't win."

"Try it this way," Corgan told them, and grinning, he turned on the gravity. They fell to the deck at once, arms and legs tangled and heads bumping.

"That was bratty!" Sharla shouted, and to Ananda, "Let's get Corgan." The two girls jumped on him and began pummeling him, four fists swinging nonstop against his head, neck, and arms. This time there was no zero gravity to protect him.

"I give up! I give up!" he yelled. "Two against one. No fair! Call a cease-fire!"

Cyborg's face surfaced suddenly in the stairwell from the galley. "What's happening up here?" he demanded. "I keep hearing all this thumping. Did something break?"

"Just Corgan's head," Ananda answered.

"We were having a weighty discussion," Sharla told him. "Or maybe it was weightless."

"Is everyone okay?" Cyborg asked.

"Oh, yes," both Ananda and Sharla answered. "Corgan may be a bit brain-damaged," Sharla added, "but it's hard to tell because he always acts that way."

"Hah! It's only when two women come after me at once," Corgan told him. "Happens all the time. Bye-bye, Cyborg. See you in Florida."

Ananda waved him good-bye, and Cyborg, with a last look of uncertainty, disappeared.

Corgan was glad that Delphine had fed them a big meal that morning—the spaceship's food was stored below in the galley, where Cyborg waited. Ananda seemed resigned to staying on deck now, so maybe in a couple of hours Corgan could go down and get them something to eat.

Having nothing to do but look out the port at the changing surface of Earth eventually grew tiresome for the girls. Ananda took Diva out of the cage and held her while Sharla cautiously petted the dog. "I think pregnancy is good for her," Ananda was saying. "She seems much calmer, even though her leg must still hurt."

"If she has two Demi clones, will you keep both of them?" Sharla asked.

"I haven't decided. Why? Would you want one of them?"

Sharla shook her head. "I couldn't be responsible for any living creature. Not now. I just don't know where my life is heading, or where I'll be."

So Sharla felt as uncertain about the future as Corgan did. At least that meant she wasn't totally committed to Brigand. "Hey, look down there now," he said. "That's the coastline of what used to be called California. Remember it, Sharla? We saw it before, when we flew to Nuku Hiva in the Harrier jet right after the Virtual War."

They were cruising low enough that the devastation was visible all up and down the coast. Huge, gaping holes pockmarked the landscape. Broken dams had flooded kilometers of bottomlands, turning the water green with tons of slime. Empty shells of what had once been buildings raised shattered walls. "I read that there used to be huge cities down there," Ananda said. "One of them was called Lost Angels or something like that."

"Lost Angels!" Corgan chuckled. "You're not so good at remembering city names, Ananda. A couple of months ago you told me the destroyed city closest to the Flor-DC was called Carnival. That was wrong. It was really Cape Canaveral." Right away he was sorry he'd said that—he didn't want to clue her into their destination. Not yet.

Quickly changing the subject, he asked Sharla, "Will you restore Mendor now so I can consult the program? Then come over here and figure out how to work this infrared scope. When we get close to the Wyo-DC, I'll have to start navigating full-time. You can do the infrared imaging, okay? Ananda, you watch the compass to keep me on course, and the altimeter to make sure I don't sink down through the cloud cover."

"Say 'please,'" Sharla told him.

Ananda echoed, "Yeah, say 'please.'"

Palms together in front of his face, he bowed and said, "Please." Trying to keep two girls happy was a bigger job than sailing the *Tuli* into a headwind.

In less than an hour they'd reached the airspace above the Wyoming domed city. The Earth hologram had been right; he couldn't see through the cloud cover, but he was intensely curious about the Wyo-DC's dome. Had it been sealed once both Harrier jets had flown away from the city? That's what he'd try to find out. Yet it wasn't the only reason he wanted to hover over the Wyo-DC. He had a sense of attachment to the place: It was where he'd been conceived in a test tube, gestated in a laboratory, and raised in a virtual-reality Box. Maybe he wanted to see his roots once more, even from eight kilometers high.

"Why are we doing this?" Sharla asked again.

"I'll tell you sometime," Corgan answered. "Not just now."

Ananda complained, "You're keeping Cyborg prisoner for this extra time, and you won't even give us an explanation."

"I am the commander of the *Prometheus*, and I'm not required to explain my flight plan to the crew," Corgan said with authority, or at least he hoped he sounded authoritative. "I give the orders. But I will tell you one thing—I want to gather possible evidence of what the Wyo-DC is like now that Brigand is gone." What Corgan really wanted to know was whether the rebels were in charge and running things—ruining things? Or were the citizens ready to rebel against the rebels? He hoped Mendor could pick up some sound from the dome. Mendor's instrumentation was so sensitive that he/she had once caught the rumble of a volcano erupting on an island called Japan.

As Sharla set up Mendor, Corgan marveled all over again at how the program could expand from palm size all the way to room size. But rooms were solid and real, while Mendor was mostly shimmering illusion. "You'll have to check it," Sharla said. "It's coded so it won't respond to anyone but you, Corgan. It's that iris identification thing."

Corgan stepped in front of the wavering curtains of light—they looked almost like the aurora borealis they'd passed through on their way to the space station. "Mendor, turn on," he instructed. He stood still so Mendor could check the pattern of the iris in his right eye—that took only forty-seven hundredths of a second.

"I'm here, Corgan," Mendor announced. "Thank you for taking me with you."

"No problem," Corgan said. "We're flying over the Wyo-DC right now. . . ."

"My old home," Mendor said.

"Mine too. But I don't have visual contact because of the cloud cover. I'd like you to pick up whatever sound you can, Mendor, and record it in your memory banks for analysis."

"I can do that," Mendor answered, with a face halfway between mother figure and father figure. "But may I ask why?"

Corgan sighed. "Not you too, Mendor. Just do it, okay?"

Intensely curious and standing only a few meters from him, Sharla and Ananda had been able to hear everything Corgan said, but they couldn't see Mendor or hear Mendor's words because those were beamed to a frequency wired into Corgan at birth. "Are you checking the compass?" he asked Ananda. "Look, you can enlarge the Earth hologram to monitor where we're flying. That little gold pinpoint of light shows our flight path. I want to keep circling for a while. Sharla, start focusing the infrared scope. Uh . . . please! First get some distant images, then close-ups."

"Just what in particular are you looking for?" Sharla asked.

"Whether the retractable doors in the Wyo-DC dome are operational."

"Is this part of that future planning you were talking about?"

"Possibly."

Mendor announced, "I have a fix on the domed city. Some sounds seem no different from before Brigand's revolt. I'm recording the noise of the machinery in the food factory. Also the gear shifts of the hovercar transport system. But . . . there are also screams. I hear people screaming."

That sent a jolt through Corgan. Screams could mean the rebels were torturing citizens again, the way they'd done during the revolt. "Analyze whatever you can," he told Mendor, "and record it."

Maneuvering away from the Wyo-DC, he tried to get the screams and what they implied out of his mind because he had to concentrate on navigation—he'd have time later to worry about them. He set the flight speed on slow, wanting to arrive over Florida around ten at night, when darkness would be complete.

"Let's eat," Ananda suggested. "I'll run down to the galley and get some packs of food."

"I think I better do it," he told her, and amazingly Ananda didn't argue.

Below deck he found Cyborg asleep and nudged him with a toe. "Help me grab some food packs," he told him.

Cyborg scrambled to his feet and pulled open the galley door. "You'll need water, too," he said, "to mix them with."

"There's water on deck. Listen, Cyborg," he said, whispering, hoping Brigand wasn't tuned in to Cyborg's thoughts at that precise moment, "when we land, I have to blindfold you. You can't know anything about . . . anything." Better not say more.

"I understand." Cyborg shrugged as though it didn't bother him, at least not too much. "If Ananda objects, you can tell her it's fine with me."

"Thanks, friend. I can always count on you. And . . ." Corgan shifted from foot to foot before he managed to continue. "Listen, I want to apologize for what I said that day, about scorching your circuitry—"

"Forget it," Cyborg interrupted. He gave Corgan a little punch in the shoulder that almost made him drop the food packets.

"No, I can't forget it. I had a meltdown and I acted like an ass. You gotta know, Cyborg, that no matter what happens—"

"Let it go, Corgan. We're good. You better take that food up to the girls."

Hesitating, Corgan stood before his one real friend, wanting to articulate his feelings, to tell Cyborg how grateful he was for that friendship, but Corgan hadn't been engineered to express his thoughts easily. "Right, I'm on my way," he said, and hurried up the stairs to the deck, where he found Sharla and Ananda hovering over the dog.

"Did you bring something for Diva?" Ananda asked. "I think she's starved."

"Yes, I remembered. You ought to eat too, both of you, and then get some sleep."

For once they listened to him without arguing. Maybe because he was sounding more like a commander or maybe just because they were tired, they did what he suggested for once. After they'd eaten their rations and fed the dog, they went to sleep.

Another hour passed, and Mendor suggested, "You should rest too, Corgan."

"I can't, Mendor. I have to check too many things. If I'm off by a hundredth of a degree, it'll be total disaster."

"Shall I relax you?" Mendor asked. "With soothing music?"

"I don't want to be relaxed. I need to be energized."

"I could play Delphine's favorite music from the 2060s."

"Anything but that!" Corgan cried. "I just want to talk to you."

"About?"

There was no stool for Corgan to sit on, so he stood facing the cloth that held the attentive expression Mendor wore now. He began, "Royal's grandfather talks to him in dreams, and he gave Royal a message for me. This was the message: 'If you don't lose your head, you'll win.'"

"Interesting," Mendor said, his/her pale green face rippling. "But nothing remarkable. I assume you want my interpretation."

"Yes."

"First, forecasts made in dreams are not scientific. However, I would interpret Royal's message as a general rule for life, not a specific warning. It just means that one should always remain calm and think about things logically to achieve the best results."

"What about the winning part?" Corgan wanted to know.

"Be in control and you're sure to win success."

"That's it? I thought it might be about a showdown between me and Brigand, because everyone keeps telling me how much he wants to kill me." With a shiver he remembered those screams coming from the Wyo-DC. "And I so much want to see him squirm and suffer for all the terrible things he's done to people, in both Wyoming and Florida."

Mendor suggested, "Shall I bring up your old skill-building games—Golden Bees, and Precision and Sensitivity Training? You can sharpen your war skills."

Those were the games that had helped him train for a war

fought virtually with hand-size digital images of enemy sol-
diers. They wouldn't be much help in hand-to-hand combat
with a brutal Brigand, if that's what lay ahead.

But why not? "Sure, Mendor," he said. "Bring on the
Golden Bees."

Seventeen

Corgan leaned over Ananda and placed his fingertips on her lips to awaken her. When her eyes flew open, he whispered, "Shhhh," and she stayed silent. Gesturing for her to follow him, he led her halfway around the circular deck of the *Prometheus*, as far away as he could get from where Sharla sat asleep in her chair, her head resting on crossed arms. He didn't want Sharla to hear any of what he was going to say.

Ananda waited, her dark eyebrows raised inquiringly as Corgan murmured, "We're getting close to Florida. I need to give you the details of the plan, but you have to promise that you won't repeat any of this to Sharla or Cyborg."

"You're going to tell me and not Sharla?" Maybe it was the intensity of his eyes and voice that made Ananda quickly agree, "Okay, I promise."

"Here's the deal, Ananda. I never told you or anyone about this, but Thebos's old laboratory, where he worked at Cape Canaveral, is connected by a two-mile tunnel to the underground chamber of the Flor-DC."

"*The* tunnel," Ananda said, nodding.

"Yeah. You saw the door to the tunnel the day we were in the underground chamber—"

"I remember. When you opened the door, Demi sneezed,

so we thought there was contamination inside and we didn't go in."

"Right. Well, that's where we're going to land," he told her.

"In the tunnel?"

"Ananda, get real! I couldn't park this big spaceship inside a tunnel. Look, I'll explain, but I have to talk fast. Thebos built the *Prometheus* in his laboratory at Cape Canaveral. Then after the devastation he dug that tunnel from his lab to the Florida domed city—it took him seven years. When it was finished, he dismantled the *Prometheus* and carried it piece by piece through the tunnel into that concealed upper floor inside the Flor-DC. That's where he put the spaceship back together."

"In that secret room we flew out of?"

"Correct. Okay, here's the important part: A little while later the roof of his entire laboratory back at Cape Canaveral collapsed, because it was weak from the nuclear attack maybe, so now there's nothing there but a big crater."

"The bomb crater you were talking about. I'm getting the picture."

"Uh-huh. So we'll land in the crater, and we'll go through the tunnel to the Flor-DC."

"Brilliant!" She smiled. "And Brigand doesn't know about the tunnel?"

"I'm . . . pretty sure he doesn't." Staring straight into Ananda's eyes, he put his hands on her shoulders and said, "You absolutely must not even hint at any of this to Cyborg, because he's sharp and he'll figure it out if you breathe a word, and then it goes straight to Brigand's foul brain."

"My lips are sealed," she promised.

"And Cyborg has to be blindfolded while Sharla leads him through the tunnel. The whole time."

Nodding, Ananda said, "So that's why you didn't want Sharla to hear all this, because you don't want her to spill any hints to Cyborg. Okay. What's my job?"

"You'll help me carry the Locker through the tunnel. I don't want to leave it in the *Prometheus* because . . . I'll tell you why later."

Corgan hadn't mentioned all the things that could go wrong. The most serious one: He'd have to navigate toward a landing in total darkness because from as far away as twenty kilometers any lights on the *Prometheus* could be spotted from the Florida dome. Brigand would already know, from reading Cyborg's mind, that the *Prometheus* was on its way, and he'd have lookouts posted around every section of the dome. But the one thing Brigand didn't know about—Corgan fervently hoped!—was the existence of the tunnel.

After Sharla woke up, Corgan asked her to repack Mendor. Like Ananda, Sharla seemed to sense the seriousness of their situation, and without question she hurried to follow orders. All of them were tense as the *Prometheus* descended through the thick, humid Florida atmosphere. "We gotta turn out the spacecraft lights now," Corgan announced. "In about thirteen minutes we'll be close enough that they'd see our interior lights if we left them on."

The night had never seemed so black, with barely enough ambient starlight to make out shapes on the ground. Corgan had no trouble observing the lighted Florida dome, but the crater where Thebos's laboratory had once existed was totally invisible. As the *Prometheus* drifted forward like a ghost ship, with no illumination except the very dim numbers that barely showed up on the monitors, Corgan wished he had levers or toggle switches instead of touch screens to control flight. If he could grip something, it might ease his tension.

The crater where he wanted to land was located two miles—3.2 kilometers—from the dome, the exact length of the tunnel that connected the two points. Where the roof of the laboratory had collapsed inward there should be no trees growing, no growth of any kind, just rubble. "Ananda," he said, "look down. Can you see any trees?"

"I can hardly see anything. Trees? Mmm, maybe."

He told her, "Look for a place that *doesn't* have trees."

"It's pretty hard to see in the dark . . ."

"I know."

"But I think over there . . ." She pointed.

Ananda was right, there were no trees, but there was a pond instead. Corgan managed to gain altitude just before he would have landed belly-down in the water. "We'll search again," he said through clenched teeth.

They hovered, almost unmoving, until Ananda said, "Down there. No trees, and I see some shapes like broken walls."

Corgan gave thanks that Thebos had engineered the *Prometheus* so flawlessly it didn't stall out when it barely moved. "We're just two meters aboveground," Sharla called out.

With the *Prometheus* suspended beneath the rim that surrounded the pit, Corgan turned on landing lights, but on only the bottom of the craft. He kept them dim, just bright enough to confirm that they'd found the crater. After the spacecraft had settled gently onto the ground, Corgan cut the motor and dropped his face forehead-down onto the control panel, his arms hanging lifeless, his breathing shallow. Total relief. He'd made it.

"Well done," Sharla murmured, hugging him.

Then they heard Cyborg say, "I can tell we landed. Can I come up now?"

"Yes, but you don't know where we are," Corgan told him for Brigand's benefit.

Although Corgan was aware they needed to move ahead with the next step, he could hardly force himself to stand up. He was drained, not by failure, but by success. Cyborg and Ananda waited silently while Sharla rubbed Corgan's shoulders. "You were totally amazing," she told him.

"Thanks," he said weakly. "We should start out now." With effort he got to his feet and said, "Ananda, we'll carry Diva's cage on top of the Locker. Sharla, you lead Cyborg." And to Cyborg, "Sorry, friend," as he untied the strip of tapa cloth from around Sharla's waist and wound it across Cyborg's eyes, making sure he couldn't see a thing. "I'm taking two portable lights from the *Prometheus*," he told them, "one for me and one for you, Sharla, so we can tell where we're going. But Cyborg stays blindfolded, and you can't say a word to Cyborg about what you're seeing, Sharla. Got that?"

"I understand," she said. "Maybe I'll recite poetry to him."

"Just keep quiet," Corgan ordered. "Don't talk at all. It's safer that way. Cyborg, try to keep your mind blank. Don't even connect to any messages from your feet about what's underneath your steps. Okay, Sharla, help Cyborg . . ." He was about to say "help Cyborg get out of the *Prometheus* and climb down to the ground," but even that simple comment could channel information to Brigand. Instead Corgan gestured, not using words.

After they'd all disembarked, Corgan and Ananda unloaded the Locker and the dog cage. Standing silently in the rubble-filled pit, Corgan swung his light around, remembering how he'd found the monitors here in boxes half covered with dirt. The crater's crumbled walls reached several meters higher than the top of the spaceship, and now, for the first time in decades, the *Prometheus* stood once again in the place where it had been created, back in those pre-devastation years, when this was a real laboratory and not a bombed-out hole.

Quickly Corgan shone the light on the door to the tunnel. He wanted to get his group out of there before they inhaled too much contaminated air. A person could breathe a certain amount of dangerous pollution without immediate ill effects, but this deep pit might have collected additional particles from nuclear fallout.

He pried open the door that led to the tunnel, then gestured for Sharla and Cyborg to go first. Because of the blindfold Cyborg stumbled a bit, but Sharla supported him by holding his arm. Once inside the tunnel Corgan began to worry because whatever happened next could be out of his control, determined by chance, that favorite concept of Delphine's. "Fall back a little bit," he muttered to Ananda, shifting his hand to relieve the pressure from the Locker they were carrying. "I want to tell you the rest of what you have to do, and I don't want them to hear."

After she'd slowed down, he told her, "Here's the deal. When we get to the end of the tunnel, you'll go through the door and seal it with mud so it looks undisturbed. Then you sneak up to the main level—I mean really sneak, like, being as invisible as you can. Try to reach Thebos. Tell him we're here, and tell him we need a way to get to the medical center or wherever he wants us to hide."

The greatest uncertainty was whether Ananda would be able to find Thebos—would he still live in his chambers in the center? "If it turns out Thebos is in danger from Brigand," Corgan whispered, "bring him back to this tunnel, and we'll rush him to the *Prometheus* and take off for Wyoming. That's why I checked out the Wyo-DC on the way here."

"Then, why are we bothering to carry the Locker all the way through the tunnel now?" Ananda asked softly.

"Because Thebos might refuse to go to Wyoming. If he does, we can Locker him right here."

"What if he doesn't want to be Lockered?" Ananda asked.

That stopped Corgan so abruptly he almost lost his grip on the Locker. He'd never even considered that Thebos wouldn't want to be Lockered. Royal hadn't wanted to, but Royal was only fifteen. Thebos was ninety-one! Full of aches and pains and brittle bones, and short of breath and forgetful, he claimed, although Corgan thought that last part was only an act.

"Nah," Corgan disagreed, "there's no way he won't want to."

"Then, I'll do everything you've told me," Ananda said, "as long as I don't run into trouble with the guards. If that happens, I'll knock some heads."

"Just don't let Brigand know where we are!" Corgan warned.

Using his extraordinary ability to calculate time, Corgan could predict precisely when they'd reach the tunnel door— 2:40 a.m. At 2:38, after setting down the Locker, he stopped Sharla and gestured to let her know that she and Cyborg should wait where they were.

Corgan moved to the tunnel door, with Ananda following right behind him. As he reached for the handle, her hand shot out to grab his, and she whispered, "Wait!"

"What? We have to hurry."

"I think there's a big flaw in your plan," she murmured softly. "I don't think it's possible for me to get all the way to the medical center without a single person noticing me—the city is never totally empty at any time. I mean, they have street cleaners and other workers out at night, and every single person in the Flor-DC recognizes me. I'm a celebrity here. They'll know I've been missing for a few weeks, and if they spot me, they'll get excited and tell the newspeople right away, and Brigand will find out."

His hand froze on the door handle. What Ananda had said was true. Everyone knew her, and for her to move through the underground chamber, up the elevator, and through the streets to the medical center without being seen was chancy at best.

"You're right," Corgan told her. "Change of plans—you stay here with Sharla and Cyborg, but don't say anything Cyborg can hear. I'll go and get Thebos myself."

"Just be careful," Ananda warned.

Corgan opened the door a crack to peer through it. The underground chamber was dark and seemed empty, so he opened the door wider. After he'd slipped through and

Ananda had pulled the door shut behind him, he stood in total darkness for a few seconds, wondering if he should turn on the handheld light but deciding against it. Fumbling in the dark, he felt the outline of the door and began to scoop up dirt to fill the cracks so they wouldn't be visible.

The light, when it blazed, blinded him. As he whirled around, all he could see was a fist holding a thick club that came smashing down on him. Then . . . nothing.

Eighteen

"If you don't lose your head, you'll win." Royal's voice echoed in Corgan's not quite conscious mind. Corgan knew he hadn't lost his head because it hurt so much. As his eyes slowly opened, he tried to reconstruct what had happened, and when. He remembered a sudden bright light and a club streaking down. . . . From the way his head hurt, he must have been bashed pretty hard. He wondered if his skull was cracked.

Where was he now? He saw only four gray walls surrounding a floor smaller than his old virtual-reality Box back in Wyoming.

Where were Sharla, Ananda, and Cyborg? Were they still in the tunnel, or had they been found and pulled out and beaten too? Surely Brigand wouldn't have let his guards hurt them—he had no quarrel with anyone but Corgan. Most likely they hadn't killed Corgan right away because Brigand was saving that pleasure for himself.

He couldn't tell how much time had passed since he got whacked. Crawling on his knees, he reached a wall and sat against it, rubbing his head where it throbbed. As his brain cleared a bit, he looked around again. Bare walls, floor, and ceiling, no glimmer from a light source, and yet he was able to see. But there was nothing to look at. Never in his life had he been so totally without sensory information of any kind. Here there was nothing visual, nothing audible, or even olfactory, like the smell of a jungle. He could feel the floor and the walls, but they communicated nothing, not the slightest vibration that might indicate something was moving outside. No door, no window, just blankness. This was total emptiness.

At first he thought he might be hallucinating, but a tray full of food seemed to glide slowly through one of the walls, becoming visible a centimeter at a time, like a virtual image. When he crawled over to the tray, he found that it was real and that the wall behind it, when he touched it, felt solid. How the devil had the tray moved through that impenetrable wall?

He poked at the food, fake food made from soybeans mostly, but that was what he'd grown up on, and he ate it because there was nothing better to do except count the minutes and seconds, waiting for something to happen. Apparently his time-splitting ability hadn't been erased by the blow to his head, but he still didn't know the actual hour of day.

Three hours and nineteen minutes after he'd started counting, Sharla and Ananda suddenly appeared through the same wall, and again their entrance port vanished instantly. As they rushed to him and hugged him, he asked, confused, "Are you in jail too? Is your cell on the other side of mine?"

"No, we're not locked up," Sharla answered, looking worried about his condition. "Are you all right? Let me see your head. You're not bleeding, but there's a big lump."

"I'm so terribly terribly sorry," Ananda cried. "I swear we

didn't speak a word inside the tunnel, and I don't know how the guards caught you, but somehow they must have known you were there. I guess they could see the outline of the tunnel door 'cause you didn't have time to hide it, so they pried it open and pulled us out."

All that planning, all that caution, all for nothing. Discouraged, Corgan leaned back against the wall and asked, "If you two aren't locked up, where did Brigand put you?"

"We're sharing Ananda's rooms in the city," Sharla answered.

Ananda added, "Everything there is just the way I left it. Nothing has been touched, not my clothes or my shoes. . . ." Choking up a little, she added, "Even Demi's dog dish is still there, in the same place it always was."

"And Cyborg's in the apartment on the other side," Sharla was saying. "You're the only one in jail, Corgan, and we all feel horrible about it."

Not as horrible as Corgan felt. "What about Thebos?" he asked. "Is he all right?"

"Yes. He'll come to see you as soon as he can sneak in here," Sharla answered in a rush. "Thebos is just amazing. We were terrified when Brigand declared you an enemy of the revolt and ordered you executed, but Thebos came up with this great idea to stage a face-off battle between you and Brigand. It'll be a spectator sport, Corgan against Brigand, with all the citizens invited."

"But not a fight to the death," Ananda said, "thanks to Thebos. He convinced Brigand."

It was hard to take in all this news, especially with his head throbbing. "You've seen Brigand, Sharla?"

Nodding, she said, "And he isn't sixteen, he's grown up. He did not get Lockered long distance by telepathy, like we thought he might have. He's about twenty-two now, and he's big and brawny and strong, so it's a huge relief that Thebos talked him out of a fight to the death with you."

Corgan's pride withered a little because he'd always believed he could defeat Brigand in a fair fight. But he knew he should be grateful. Since he still felt dizzy from the blow to his head, he stayed sitting on the floor, and the girls sat beside him, cross-legged, one on each side.

One more question swept into Corgan's consciousness. "The Locker! Did Brigand get the Locker?"

Sharla answered, "Like I said, that Thebos is an amazing guy. He was right there when the New Rebel Troopers brought the Locker up from the tunnel, and he managed to slip a dual-core processor out of the mechanism. Then he told Brigand that it must have been damaged during the flight, and he'd have to fix it later. Oh, there's so much to tell you, so much going on out there!"

"But Brigand doesn't know we're visiting you," Ananda reported. "We're being super careful so he won't find out, but he's so busy trying to run the world he doesn't have much time for anything else right now, and that includes Sharla. He got rid of the Supreme Councils, both here and in Wyoming, and no members of the New Rebel Troops know anything about governing. So everything's a mess out there. Things are breaking down everywhere."

Corgan took a deep breath. "So, what's next? What am I supposed to do now? How long is Brigand going to keep me in this cell?"

Ananda and Sharla both looked concerned. "We don't know," Sharla said.

"We're just lucky we got in here to talk to you. We're not supposed to be here—we had to bribe the guard to get in," Ananda added.

"There's a guard outside?"

"Yeah," Sharla answered. "Big, rough-looking guy."

"With shoulders like boulders," Ananda added. "Which matches his head, because he has about as much brains as a rock."

At that the two girls laughed a little, smacking each other's palms.

"How'd you bribe him?" Corgan wanted to know.

Casually, as if the topic weren't too important, Ananda answered, "I told you I'm a celebrity in the Flor-DC. I promised to give him an autographed holographic image of me."

Months ago Corgan had seen how much the Flor-DC citizens loved Ananda. They not only admired her as the strongest, most athletic woman anywhere, they felt protective of her because they knew about the tragedy that had killed her parents when she was only two.

Sharla told him, "Try to get over that lump on the head and let us figure things out, Corgan. We've got the best minds in the world working for you—Cyborg and Thebos. That's what's giving us hope. We'd better leave now before Cyborg starts wondering where we are and Brigand channels him, and you know how that goes. Good-bye, Corgan. Please do everything to stay safe. I promise you we're doing all we can to keep you alive."

"Wait! Before you go, can you tell me the actual time?

What time is it now, and how long have I been in here?" He needed a set point to get his timing ability in sync again.

"You've been here thirteen hours, seven minutes, and twenty-seven seconds," Ananda answered. "Remember, I'm a time-splitter too. And right now it's four thirty-nine p.m. plus some inconsequential seconds."

When they disappeared, Corgan leaped at the wall and tried to figure out how it could vaporize like that to allow things through it and then turn rock solid again in microseconds. He ran his hands over the whole surface and felt nothing. The wall seemed as impenetrable as steel. Feeling weak again, he sank to his knees.

And then the awareness slowly swept over him. Sharla had come to see *him*. She'd connected with Brigand, but she'd managed to get away from him to come to Corgan. And she'd conspired with Cyborg and Thebos to help Corgan. Sharla was on his side—against Brigand!

He stretched on the floor with his arms over his head, letting it sink in and trying to evaluate. Was he right? Had she really chosen him over Brigand?

Then he rose to his feet. If his friends were trying to set up a fair, impartial, aboveboard match to keep him alive, he'd better do his part. The dizziness was still there. With one hand against the wall he walked the periphery of the cell, staggering a little at first, but concentrating to keep his balance. Then he walked it again without holding on, again and again, going faster each time, until he could stay balanced even with his eyes closed.

After precisely one hour he lay on the floor to sleep. In this confined cell there was no way to tell day from night, no brightening or dimming of the light, so he set up an hourly training schedule to make himself strong. It came into his mind that if his jailers watched him training, they might try to sabotage him by not letting him sleep, but that didn't happen. No lights shone in his eyes, no loud noises bombarded his ears, and the floor, although hard, didn't get cold.

When he awoke in the morning, his breakfast was already there, sitting in the corner, bland but wholesome. Even better, he found a wet cloth he could wash himself with and a bottle of Nutri-Build, the same drink Mendor had given him when he was preparing for the Virtual War. Who was putting these things into his cell?

Another day went by, and he could feel himself grow stronger. Where was Thebos? There was nothing in his cell to distract him, so Corgan's entire attention centered on his body, his reflexes, his speed. And beyond that—his tactics.

Brigand must have an artificial knee. Most likely Thebos had built one for him after Brigand's knee got shot off in their last battle. How could Corgan take advantage of that? He practiced kicking at the height of Brigand's knees until he got so fast he couldn't see his own foot swing, just a blur.

During the breaks he allowed himself he sat on the floor and stared at the wall in front of him, trying to figure out how it dissolved and instantly reformed when something came through it. His jailers were smart—they never sent the food tray through the same spot or at precisely the same hour. Corgan could sit there concentrating on a section of the wall, waiting to pounce, and the food tray would slip through at the other end of the wall before he could reach it, with the wall solidifying behind it fast enough that even Corgan's time-splitting ability couldn't get a grip on it. Only once did he almost make it. When he saw the edge of the tray skim inside, he shot out his arm and hit the mark so quickly that his fingers penetrated two centimeters before the wall hardened, sending such a jolt of pain through his fingertips that he decided he wouldn't try that again.

The next day Thebos arrived suddenly, his pale, sunken eyes brightening with affection as his shaky fingers grasped Corgan's shoulders. Corgan had to remind himself not to squeeze too hard when they hugged each other, but he was overjoyed to see the old man.

"Dear boy," Thebos murmured. "I am so relieved that you returned safely. And I am so deeply touched that you came back to this city because you were worried about me."

As Thebos's eyes filled with tears, Corgan felt his own eyes stinging. "Are you well? Are you okay?" Corgan asked. "I was afraid Brigand would work you to death."

"Oh . . . Brigand," Thebos answered scornfully with a wave of his hand. "I've been putting on my doddering-old-fool act for Brigand so he doesn't expect much of me. I use a cane, I shuffle, I speak slowly and forget what I'm saying halfway through—it works." As Thebos related that, a chair slipped through the wall for him. Corgan wanted to ask how it was done, that in-and-out-of-the-wall technique, but he might not have much time with Thebos. When the old man sank into the chair, Corgan slid to his knees in front of him, like a penitent asking for a blessing.

"What about the Locker?" Corgan asked. "Will you use it to get young again? Sharla said you disabled it, but you could fix it, and Cyborg could take you back to whatever age you want."

Thebos arranged himself more comfortably in the chair. "Later perhaps. I don't want to fix the Locker now because Brigand would demand to be Lockered, and I don't want him to live forever. He's completely immoral—he should not become immortal."

"Maybe I'll take care of that," Corgan said.

As though he hadn't heard, Thebos continued to speak, drumming his gnarled fingers on the chair arm. "The match between you two will be a great spectacle for the crowds to watch. Since Brigand seized power and things started falling apart, he's been keeping the masses entertained by spectacles— the old bread-and-circuses concept. That was a ploy of the ancient Roman emperors."

Corgan, as so often happened, had trouble following Thebos's meaning.

"Your dual combat," Thebos went on, "your conflict, battle, match, whatever you want to call it—Brigand is now hell-bent on staging it. He desires it to be a public perform-ance with the largest possible audience. And whatever Brigand wants, Brigand gets. For the moment."

Corgan considered that. It would be weird to fight in front of a crowd, but it seemed he didn't have a choice. "Just make sure he doesn't oil his body this time. The last time we fought he was so greased up I couldn't get a good hold on him."

Before he'd finished saying that, Thebos started to shake his head. "No, no, no," he protested. "It's not going to be that way at all. No physical contact. It will all be virtual reality. A new kind of Virtual War."

"What?"

"We devised this so cleverly," Thebos congratulated himself. "Cyborg and I. I know engineering and Cyborg knows his clone-twin better than anyone else does. So we're creating these huge virtual images of you and Brigand, about nine feet tall. There will be a line drawn between the two images that neither of them can step across. You and Brigand will be strapped into wired chairs facing each other, but you'll be seated behind your virtual avatars—"

"Virtual!" Corgan gasped.

"Let me finish! You will control the movement of your avatars entirely through your thoughts, because you will be unable to move in the chairs. Think of it, Corgan! A battle controlled only by brain waves. Each of the large images of you and Brigand will be mathematically divided into one hundred sections. As one avatar hits the other, it will take out one section at a time. One hundred blows to destroy an avatar completely, or fewer if you strike a strategic area like the eyes or brain or heart, which will stop your opponent cold."

Corgan could hardly comprehend. "You mean we'll be strapped into chairs and have to move these big images of ourselves *mentally*?"

"Exactly."

"What about the fight-to-the-death part?"

"We've worked it out this way: The winner," Thebos announced, "will decide the fate of the loser. That creates endless possibilities for a thrilling finale."

"I don't like this idea!" Corgan cried, clenching his fists. "Brigand will find some way to make it look like he won."

"Calm down, Corgan! Cyborg and I will watch every move like hawks. We've been brainstorming this ever since you got back. This is by far the safest scenario for you. If you enter into physical combat, you'll lose, because Brigand is a full-grown man now and you're still a youth. Brigand is taller than you and he outweighs you. Give us credit for thinking up this ingenious scheme to offer you a chance!"

"No!" Corgan argued. "I can take him. I've been training."

Thebos gave a little snort, but not of laughter. "Don't delude yourself, Corgan. You haven't seen Brigand lately. He's bulked up like Goliath. And you're just a David. But you don't understand that reference either, do you? Don't you see? We're trying to save your life."

Raising his head, Corgan declared, "If I die in a real fight, at least I'll die with honor."

"Spoken like a teenage idiot," Thebos scoffed. "The whole idea is for you *not* to die at all." Thebos leaned forward, his watery gray eyes staring straight into Corgan's. "Listen to me, Corgan. You have to wonder why Brigand would even agree to a contest where so much is at stake for him. The answer is that he's supremely confident he'll win. He's an adult now, with a mature brain, and he's a strategist. We've assured him that the contest will be scrupulously fair, and he believes that because his clone-twin is part of the team, so he can check up on Cyborg mentally whenever he wants. What does he have to fear? Nothing! At least as he sees it."

Corgan felt a chill in his chest as Thebos's words sank in.

"On the other hand," Thebos went on, "you spent the first fourteen years of your life training for a virtual war. Some of your skills may have become a bit rusty, but those skills can resurface, I'm confident of that. They're an intricate part of

you. They're in your genes. But . . . regardless of the out-
come, you don't need to worry. If Brigand defeats you, I'm
working on a plan that will whisk you away so you'll be safe
from harm."

Corgan rose to his feet, trying to untangle his thoughts.
He knew his friends were attempting to save his life, but he
didn't want to come off as a coward. "I'm not happy about
this, Thebos. It's just another way for me to run away from
Brigand again."

Thebos stood up too, shakily. "Once you think things
through, you'll realize that this solution is an excellent one.
But now I must go, before I'm missed."

Thebos turned and shuffled—the shuffling was real, not
pretense, Corgan noticed. When the wall atomized to let him
through, Corgan moved so fast he pushed Thebos and himself into it simultaneously, managing to catch Thebos upright
on the other side and set him on his feet. "What are you
doing?" Thebos cried.

"I'm breaking out," Corgan yelled, throwing his fist into
the guard's throat.

Thebos pleaded, "Corgan, wait!" but Corgan was running
and the guard was sinking to the ground, clutching his throat.

Corgan recognized instantly where he was—he was
familiar with the entire layout of the Flor-DC. He'd had
plenty of time to explore it when he'd taken Ananda's dog for
walks. Finding his way easily now, he raced toward the center
of the city, noticing as he ran that the streets were littered with
trash and that people stood around talking when they should
have been at their jobs.

He reached the building where the Supreme Council had

met, but the elevator didn't operate, so he ran up the stairs three at a time. If Brigand had executed the whole Council, their empty quarters might be a place Corgan could hide while he sorted out what was happening and planned his next move. But the door to the room was locked.

Frustrated, he ran back down into the street. He'd try to make it to Ananda's rooms and stay there until nightfall, when he could sneak into the medical center with Thebos. He ran toward the moving walkway and leaped over its wall. The second he cleared it he realized the walkway wasn't working, even though he could hear the motor running. The impact sent a jolt of electricity through him, stunning him, and before he could get up again, a dozen New Rebel Troopers surrounded him.

"The shortest escape in history," one of the troopers sneered.

Nineteen

"Make sure all this is recorded," Brigand was saying to some-one near him. "I want it to be broadcast, but not until after I edit it."

The words didn't register with Corgan, who was strug-gling against the New Rebel Troopers, three on each side of him. At first he'd barely noticed where he was, but when he finally quit struggling, he looked up to see Brigand seated on what looked like a throne—large and gilded with carvings of the same sharks' teeth, sunbursts, snakes, scorpions, and death heads that he had tattooed all over his torso. His chest tattoos were visible, too; he wore a shirt of shimmering transparent cloth that let all his grotesque markings show through.

The tattoo on the left side of his face, from the middle of his forehead down the center of his nose to his chin, looked a little different now because Brigand's face had broadened at the forehead and the jawline. His chin was firmer, his cheek-bones more visible, his red eyebrows were thicker, and his eyes seemed set slightly deeper, but the most startling thing about his new appearance was his size.

"Bulked up" was what Thebos had said about Brigand. Big was what Corgan noticed—in height, in the wide shoulders, the arms with bulging muscles, and the deep chest. Corgan couldn't help thinking about sixteen-year-old Cyborg and comparing him with this grown-up version of him. Was this the body Cyborg would have grown into if he hadn't been Lockered? How did Cyborg feel when he saw this adult Brigand; what was it like knowing he'd never be as brawny as this, or as strong as this, no matter how long he lived?

They stared at each other, Corgan defiant, Brigand with an expression of scornful amusement. "So, you came back," Brigand finally said. "You must have missed me a lot."

"It was the bullet that missed you, unfortunately," Corgan said. "Too bad it shot off your knee instead of your head."

One of the New Rebel Troopers looked ready to gut-punch Corgan for that taunt, but Brigand raised his hand. "No, don't crush the little worm. We'll keep him intact for the skirmish."

As Brigand spoke, he didn't quite meet Corgan's eyes; his face turned just slightly to the left. Corgan glanced in that direction and saw the wide lens of a visualizer trained on the scene. It seemed Brigand wanted this whole preliminary encounter recorded, probably so he could drum up enthusiasm for the coming match.

"You're not very smart, you know," Brigand told him. "We discovered that tunnel entrance weeks ago. We kept it guarded so none of our political prisoners could escape through it, but mainly because we figured you'd come back." Brigand waved toward the visualizer lens and said, "Strike out that last line, men. I don't want it on the broadcast."

"Why can't we fight right now?" Corgan demanded. "We're both here in the same space—let's get it over with. I don't need any fancy virtual games to dress up our battle so the citizens can have fun watching. This is between you and me, not between you and me and the whole world."

"Listen to the little man," Brigand sneered, getting up from his throne and casually descending the three steps to the floor. Corgan noticed the slight limp, and also that Brigand's pants were *not* transparent and were tucked inside his boots. "You're trying to aggravate me so I'll destroy you right now," Brigand said. As he came closer, Corgan saw that Brigand now stood a whole head taller. "But no, I won't deprive the citizens of their coming entertainment, Corgan. In fact, because I want our match to be free of any taint of dishonesty or discrimination, I'm going to send you back to your comfortable lockup and supply you with the best food in the Flor-DC, with an airbed for comfortable sleep, and with a woman if you want one. . . ."

"Don't be obscene."

Brigand carried a small whip with a fringed end; as the New Rebel Troopers held Corgan tight, Brigand swept the fringe across Corgan's face, tickling him on the lips. Corgan jerked back and spit, but Brigand quickly moved out of the way. "Such disgusting manners," Brigand said, turning toward the visualizer lens. "And troopers, make sure you put some kind of body-cleansing mechanism in his cell. He smells bad."

At that moment Cyborg rushed into the room, panting. "Hey, Brigand, do you need a negotiator here? The rules for the face-off say there shouldn't be any preliminary harassment."

"Tell that to your undisciplined little friend," Brigand answered as he turned and headed toward the steps of his throne. "He tried to spit at me."

"Hey, undisciplined little friend," Cyborg said, coming

close to Corgan and grabbing him around the back of the neck with the artificial hand. "Don't go spoiling everything." As Cyborg pulled Corgan closer and gave him a light punch in the ribs with his real hand, Corgan felt something being slipped inside his LiteSuit.

"How 'bout if I take Corgan back to his cell?" Cyborg asked Brigand. "I mean, I'll accompany his guards while they escort Corgan, and we'll get him tucked in for the night. He needs his sleep and so do you, Brigand. The great face-off is less than twenty-four hours away."

Brigand stared hard at Cyborg. It was strange to observe the two of them, so identical with that flaming red hair, but now separated by an age span of six years. "You claim to be neutral, clone-twin," Brigand said. "Should I trust you?"

"Sure. I don't have to go with Corgan, I can stay here with you. It's your call."

"I think that would be a good call," Brigand said. "Let's invite Ananda and Sharla to join us for a little late-night supper, with lights turned low and soft music. I'll send a couple of New Rebel Troopers to bring the girls."

Corgan's muscles tensed, making the troopers tighten their hold on him. If he could have broken free, he'd have charged at Brigand right there and then, but the troopers holding him were big men, and strong. They dragged him away and back to his cell, but this time when he was shoved toward it, he could see how the entrance and exit worked. An outside switch vaporized the wall to let any object or person be propelled inside without a millimeter to spare and without a microsecond wasted before the wall turned solid again.

There really was an airbed on the floor—when did that

arrive? Instead of lying on it, Corgan kicked it in frustration. Then he remembered that Cyborg had slipped something through the neck of his LiteSuit. When Corgan pulled it out, his spirits lifted. It was Mendor, compressed into a little square box. Silently he sent thanks to Cyborg.

He'd never before tried to reconstitute Mendor. Sharla had always condensed the program and later opened it up again. Puzzled, he held the small package in his hand and shook it a little, and as he stared at it, it began to expand. "Hey, great!" he cried, but not too loudly because he didn't want to be heard. "Turn on, Mendor."

In seventeen hundredths of a second the full-blown Mendor images filled the cell, just as they had back in the Wyo-DC when Corgan thought the whole world existed only in his virtual-reality Box. Mendor's aura was now a shimmering mixture of blues and greens, the mother/father face filling one whole wall of the cell, the other walls pulsating with muted abstract designs.

"This is so much better than on Nuku Hiva," Mendor enthused, "where I had only those flimsy curtains of LiteSuit cloth to project against. Four walls are what I was designed for. How are you, Corgan?"

"Not good. But glad to see you."

Settling more into the mother image, Mendor said, "Oh, I've been having quite the adventure since you and I last spoke in the *Prometheus*. First Sharla opened me, and then she created the iris identification program for Thebos so he could communicate with me."

"With Thebos? Did you communicate with Cyborg, too?" That could have been a bad idea.

"No. It wasn't necessary. I just interfaced with Thebos. And when Thebos and I had finished—with input from Sharla and Cyborg conveyed through Thebos—Sharla reconnected the ID to your own iris pattern, Corgan, so you and I could interface again. Smart girl." A little rose-colored glow crept into Mendor's image, which always happened when Mendor was pleased about something. "Mmm, I'm really enjoying this nice virtual-reality Box," she murmured as colors expanded in a rainbow of waves across all four walls.

"It's not a virtual-reality Box, Mendor," Corgan contradicted. "It's a jail cell. And I know I can't get out because New Rebel Troopers are standing guard outside."

"Jail cell or not, it works fine for me. Look, there's your dinner tray." Mendor's face slid back into the nurturing-mother persona. "I want you to eat all of it, Corgan, because it's nourishing and you'll need all your strength."

"Why? I won't even be able to land a punch on that son of a—"

"You'll need your mental strength. Now, start eating and I'll explain what has been happening."

Some of it Corgan already knew, or had figured out. It was Thebos who'd thought up the virtual-war concept, quickly approved by Brigand because he knew it would appeal to the citizens.

"It shouldn't be called a virtual war, Mendor," Corgan broke in. "It's not between the three worldwide federations, it's just a fight between two people, me and Brigand."

"Brigand wants to call it that. You were the hero of the first Virtual War, Corgan; he wants to be the hero of the second. Let him have his little ego trip."

"Little! I don't consider that little."

"Brigand's in charge here in the Flor-DC. He's the ultimate authority. Nothing happens unless he approves it. Your confrontation will be a public challenge. He loves crowds," Mendor went on, "and feeds on their adulation. I'm told he makes speeches where he throws out prizes just to hear people cheer. And that, dear Corgan, will be a problem. Have you thought . . ."

At this Mendor's image began to change into the stern father, the colors darker and more somber. "Have you thought how distracting that will be for you? All that cheering and applause? You will be trying to focus your mental energy on your avatar's movements. A shrieking crowd will break your concentration. Brigand's used to crowd noises, but you're not."

Corgan paused in his eating, although he was enjoying the food, which was real and delicious. "Mendor, you're not remembering the first Virtual War. I was bombarded with sounds—people screaming when they got blown up, land mines exploding, aircraft roaring right over my head—and I didn't lose my concentration."

Mendor's color grayed a little more, a sign that he didn't like to be argued with. "That first Virtual War seemed entirely real, but subconsciously you knew that every sound and image was nothing more than an electronic creation. During this new virtual war real people will surround you, stomping and cheering and booing and, who knows, maybe throwing things at you. This will be distracting, to say the least."

"So what are you saying, Mendor? That I can't do it?"

"No. I'm saying we have about twenty-two hours to work

on your powers of concentration. You do have one advantage. Brigand has never developed the kind of self-discipline you had when you trained for the first Virtual War. But Brigand has the genes of a supreme strategist, so he has that particular advantage over you."

Corgan had finished eating, and he shoved the tray against the wall, not caring anymore about the mechanism through which the tray disappeared. "Mendor, I don't understand something," he said.

"What is that?"

"You said Thebos and Cyborg put together the rules and everything about the contest, and Sharla and Thebos designed the program."

"That is correct." Mendor's color brightened a little, out of interest in where this might be heading.

"So if everyone's so crazy determined to keep me alive, why didn't they just tip the program so I could win?"

Mendor seemed to withdraw, his face becoming larger, sterner, and darker. "You surprise me, Corgan. In fact, I'm quite shocked. What you just asked would be . . . *dishonorable*."

Corgan felt the blood rise to his cheeks. "I'm sorry, Mendor. My brain must have flipped. Maybe it was that whack on the head."

"You were raised to respect virtue, integrity, decency, morality—"

"Mendor, please stop! I do respect them, and I said I was sorry." Corgan didn't know whether to get down on his knees to apologize or just turn off Mendor's program. "It was a stupid thing for me to say, and you've ragged on me enough, so give it a rest, Mendor."

"Remember the oath you spoke every day when you were training for the first Virtual War?"

"Sure, I remember it."

"Recite it now," Mendor demanded.

Corgan stood up straight and raised his right hand. "'I pledge to wage the War with courage, dedication, and honor.' You really think Brigand is going to play by those rules, Mendor?"

"We can't do anything about Brigand, who is entirely *dis*honorable," Mendor answered. "We can keep *your* honor intact. And don't forget for a second that honor matters more than life."

Once, Corgan had believed that. Did he still? Maybe, but lately there was a lot more he wanted to live for. He now belonged to a group of friends who really cared about him: Cyborg, Ananda, Thebos—and Sharla. Especially Sharla. His confidence in Sharla kept growing.

"Stop your dreaming!" Mendor ordered. "It's time to practice." Following Mendor's directions, Corgan took a spoon from the dinner tray and placed it two meters in front of him. Then, as instructed, he stood with his back against the wall.

"This is what you must do," Mendor told him. "We don't have your virtual avatar to practice on, but if you can manage to move this spoon using only your thought waves, you'll be able to control the avatar. Concentrate!"

Corgan stared at the spoon, blocking out everything else in his line of vision. Once, he'd been able to move digital figures without touching them by bringing his hand to within two hundred microns of an image and using his own electromagnetic energy as a force for motion. But those were digital images. This was an actual object, made of photons and electrons but having mass and occupying space. "Focus," Mendor whispered. "Focus, Corgan. Converge your brain waves into a band of pure mental energy. The narrower the better."

Corgan tried. He shut his mind to everything except Mendor's words. "The energy band is two centimeters wide," Mendor murmured. "That's too much! Compress it more. That's better. You must narrow it to one centimeter."

Corgan felt pressure build inside his skull. He became aware of the nerves that connected his eyes to his brain; he could actually see those nerves, colored blindingly bright. The sound of blood pounding in his head grew louder and louder, until he thought it would explode out of his ears. "You're getting closer," Mendor encouraged. "Focus! Try harder."

Corgan pulled the energy from every single neuron in his body, forcing it to fuse into a single luminous thought wave. Then—did he imagine it?—the spoon moved. It clattered on the floor as Corgan sank against the wall, utterly drained.

Mendor looked triumphant. "I'll bet all the electronics in my storage unit that Brigand can't do *that*!" he/she stated, morphing back to the dual-gender image because pride in a prodigy's performance was both a mother thing and a father thing. "Corgan, I am so immensely proud of you. Take a big swallow of Nutri-Build and try it again. See if you can move the spoon farther the next time."

The next time, and the next time, and the next, Corgan managed to move the spoon. Mendor was a relentless taskmaster. Or mistress. But he/she stopped the practice session right before Corgan was ready to abandon the whole contest and concede everything to Brigand.

"No, you will not surrender," Mendor ordered. "If you surrender, or if Brigand wins, he has the right to choose your fate. Do you want to let him make that choice?"

Corgan mentally ran over all the tortures Brigand might choose to exterminate him with. Death by being thrown into the toxic waters of the Atlantic, an ocean full of monstrous mutations that would love to shred a human and eat him. Or death by being stripped naked, hung upside down in the city center, and stoned by the citizens. Or death by having his body parts chopped off one by one. Whatever death Brigand chose for Corgan, it would be brutal and spectacular so the masses could watch and be entertained, unless they couldn't stop puking.

Twenty

With Mendor surrounding him on all four walls, Corgan got prodded to practice, to eat properly, to sleep enough, and to focus, focus, focus, until he got so tired of the word "focus" he started reversing the letters in his mind to "suc-off."

One hour before the battle was scheduled to start, his brain felt like a jangling mass of biological neurons tangled with invasive electronic filaments. At that moment a brand-new LiteSuit of translucent material appeared in his cell.

"It's blue!" Mendor exclaimed. "Your favorite color. You can put it on right now, because while you slept, I cleansed you all over, but gently, so you wouldn't wake up."

Corgan hoped it was Mendor the Father who'd cleansed him, not Mendor the Mother. When he lived in his old virtual-reality Box in the Wyo-DC, he wouldn't have worried about such things, but now he was older and more squeamish.

After he got dressed, Mendor bombarded him with last-chance instructions for thirty-seven minutes and fourteen hundredths of a second, then stopped. "Your muscles are awfully tense," he/she said.

"What did you expect? I might be going to my death."

"Corgan!" Mendor protested. "All your friends are trying to prevent that." In the next breath Mendor murmured sooth-ingly, "Let me massage those knots out of your muscles."

Because Mendor was the most advanced program in the world, he/she managed to knead every muscle in Corgan's body all at the same time. It definitely helped. He felt better until four New Rebel Troopers appeared, entering through the wall.

"Time to go," one of them said. "You must be mental. We heard you talking to yourself for the last twenty-four hours."

"Wouldn't you be mental if you had to fight Brigand?" another trooper asked. "'Cause this kid's gonna lose, and we know what Brigand's Instrument of Fate is." He started to laugh.

"What are you talking about?" Corgan demanded. "What Instrument of Fate?"

"It's what Brigand's gonna use on you when he wins," the fourth trooper explained, "because the rules say the winner gets to decide the fate of the loser."

Growing alarmed, Corgan asked, "What's my Instrument of Fate for Brigand if I win?"

"How should we know?" The trooper shrugged. "If you didn't already get one, I guess you don't have any. But you really don't need one, because you're gonna lose. Come on, now. Move!" They grabbed him so roughly he didn't have a chance to say good-bye to Mendor, who was invisible and inaudible to the New Rebel Troopers.

Thousands of people were jammed into the city center, and another hundred thousand would be watching the challenge broadcast to all parts of the city through the visualizer. As Corgan arrived, he heard the crowds cheering, whether for Brigand or Corgan or just because of the free entertainment, there was no way to tell.

One of the guards pointed and said, "Over there is Brigand's Instrument of Fate." It stood next to the painted boundaries of the battle area. Although draped by cloth from top to bottom, it looked menacing. Nearly three meters tall, its shape was wide, bulky, and angular. Could it be a torture rack? A gallows? The troopers kept holding Corgan so tightly he wondered if he'd have to fight the war that way, with four burly punks hanging on to him.

Where was Thebos? Corgan scanned the crowd as much as possible, turning only his head because the rest of him was held immobile. He couldn't catch sight of Thebos. Maybe getting jostled in a crowd this size would have been too difficult for him, so he'd decided to watch the match on the telescreen in the medical center.

Corgan noticed Sharla and Cyborg standing on the line that divided the battle area into two halves. It didn't bother him, at least not too much, that they'd been positioned in the center between Brigand's and Corgan's positions—it made them appear neutral, he supposed. *Were* they neutral? Both of them had strong ties to both Brigand and Corgan. Yet when Sharla looked at Corgan, he could tell from her eyes that she was scared for him, that she was silently sending him her support. Cyborg, though, stared straight ahead.

To the left of Corgan hung a score panel showing black-and-white outlines of two figures he guessed were meant to be the avatars. Each of the drawings had been sectioned into a grid of one hundred blocks—those must be the areas he'd have to hit, one after the other, on the actual avatar warrior figure. Above the drawings a sign posted the scores, now showing zero and zero, with BRIGAND lettered on one side and CORGAN on the other. He wondered if the Flor-DC citizens were betting on the final score. Or maybe the citizens of all three federations were watching from all over the world, via fiber-optic cable.

There was a sudden disturbance across the square. The crowd surged apart as though cleaved by a knife, backing up in waves as the noise level rose. Brigand had arrived, and not just arrived, he'd made a grand entrance. Only when he came close to the cleared battle area did Corgan get a look at him. He had on a *cape*, for crud's sake! It swept from his shoulders almost to the floor, a gold cape decorated with stars and moons and galaxies. Who was he supposed to be—Mr. Andromeda? When he stopped, he raised his arms, pumped his fists, and turned around in a quick circle, causing the cape to swirl out around him. People cheered. Corgan felt like heaving.

Next, two heavy armchairs were carried in and set down on each end of the arena, one of them only a meter in front of Corgan. It was then that Cyborg stepped forward, and the crowd grew hushed.

"People of the Florida domed city," Cyborg began, his voice amplified so loudly it echoed three or four times. "We are here to witness a contest between Corgan, the hero of the first Virtual War, and Brigand, the ruler of the Flor-DC, with the winner to decide the fate of the loser."

Cheers erupted. These people seemed to cheer over anything, Corgan thought.

"I'm going to state the rules of the battle," Cyborg continued. "Each contestant will be strapped to a chair, unable to move. Each will be represented by an avatar—you people out there will be able to see both avatars, but Brigand will see only Corgan's, and Corgan will see only Brigand's. The two contestants will control their avatars entirely by brain waves, not by touch."

Cyborg paused, waiting for quiet. "Each avatar is two hundred forty centimeters tall, and the surfaces of both avatars have been divided evenly into one hundred sections, from head to toe and from the left side to the right side. Each division is a square that measures twelve centimeters on all four sides. When one opponent strikes another opponent, the section where the blow lands will disappear. You can follow this," Cyborg said, "by looking at the score panel up there, because when a section gets knocked out, its position on the grid will turn black."

Corgan turned to study the grids. They'd been laid out with such precision it had to be the work of Thebos. Since he didn't know whether the grid lines would be visible on the actual avatars, he tried to memorize the sections' positions— over the heart, over the eyes, and there was one over the knee he might try to hit. No, he told himself, that would be stupid. He'd be fighting a digital avatar, not the real Brigand. Brigand had a bad knee, but the avatar wouldn't. *Think logically,* he commanded himself.

Cyborg was continuing, "If a contestant knocks out all one hundred grid sections, he'll win, obviously. But he can also win if he obliterates all the vital organs of the opponent's avatar so it can't fight any longer."

That's the clue, Corgan told himself. *Go for the vital organs.* How could he tell where they were, though, if he could see only the front surface of the avatar? The eyes would be obvious, but where was the heart located? Somewhere in the chest, but according to the grid on the diagram, the left side of the chest where the heart ought to be was divided into four square sections. The heart might be behind any of them; Corgan didn't know much about anatomy. And the avatar would be moving the whole time, making it hard to zero in on any one area.

"Now the opponents will go to their chairs."

Brigand strode over to his chair. He looked commanding as he turned and smiled toward the visualizer lens.

Corgan was shoved to his chair by four New Rebel Troopers, who immediately strapped him into it. Metal bands coiled around his wrists, elbows, and biceps. Other bands bound his thighs, knees, and ankles. A softer band of some other material circled his forehead—that's where the electronics were located. If he sat perfectly still, the bands didn't hurt. That was good. It would remind him to forget his body and concentrate on his brain waves.

Cyborg was still speaking. "The battle will last as long as it takes for one avatar to be destroyed. As soon as the battle ends, the winner will announce the fate of the loser. You can see over there"—he pointed—"that Brigand's Instrument of Fate is already in place. I mean, you can't see it because it's covered up, but that's where it is."

Cyborg had started to sweat. "Uh, one more thing. We gave names to the avatars so you could keep them straight. We . . . abbreviated . . . 'Corgan's avatar' and 'Brigand's avatar.' Corgan's will be called Cavatar, and Brigand's will be called Brave."

Oh, great! Corgan thought. Brave and Cavatar? Who came

up with that? It sounded like Brigand's was a warrior and Corgan's was tooth decay.

"So," Cyborg cried out, his voice cracking, "let the games begin."

Four and three-quarters seconds rushed by before Corgan comprehended the mechanics of this battle. He was looking through the eyes of his own avatar at Brigand's, Brave, which lurched toward the center line that divided the battlefield. Brave was so grotesque that Corgan had to fight his shock at Brave's appearance. His body was half as wide as it was tall, naked except for a narrow loincloth that barely covered what it was supposed to cover. His bulging thighs looked like moldy barrels, and across his chest sinews stretched as thick as cables over blood red skin that resembled slabs of raw beef.

Worst of all was the head. Brave's forehead bulged like a gorilla's. His yellow hair hung down over his eyes like snakes, and the eyes burned like coals. Ugliest was the raging open mouth that showed pointy black teeth and a monstrous, meaty tongue. Corgan had to take in all this in a fraction of a second because Brave stood at the line, goading Corgan with roars of "Approach me, you coward!"

Concentrating his brain energy, Corgan moved Cavatar to the line. Brave's first blow hit Cavatar in the chest. When Corgan glanced at the scoreboard to see just where he'd been struck, Cavatar got hit again. That was a lesson quickly learned: Don't look at the scoreboard. He focused his energy force on a point in Brave's throat, wanting to stop the roars, but before he could strike, Brave hit Cavatar in the groin.

The crowd yelled and screamed at that, but Corgan knew he had to block out the noise and make some hits, or this battle would be over before he'd landed a single blow. Looking through Cavatar's eyes, he sent his avatar's fists swinging out—one, two, three, four hits against Brave. But then the voice of an invisible referee rang out, "Not valid. Cavatar crossed the line."

Corgan groaned inwardly. He desperately wanted to look at the scoreboard again to see if he had any points at all, so he thrust both of Cavatar's fists forward and in a fraction of a second managed to take a quick glance. Brigand seven; Corgan one. Frustrated, he groaned out loud and heard the groan come out of his own Cavatar, magnified enough to sound fearsome.

And then, like a bolt of lightning, the prophecy tore into his consciousness as powerfully as though Royal and his grandfather were standing next to him. *"If you don't lose your head, you'll win."*

That was it! He had to protect Cavatar's head. And the opposite—*destroy Brave's head*! Electrified, Corgan let out another roar, which slowed Brave for seven tenths of a second, enough for Cavatar to land two more hits, one to Brave's cheek and the other to his forehead. The crowd yelled. This was more like it. Corgan was just about to hit him again when Brave's hoarse, gravelly voice yelled, "Watch your eyes."

Instinctively Corgan raised Cavatar's hands in front of his eyes to protect them, but instead of going for the eyes, Brave hit Cavatar in the chest. Corgan had been suckered! *Never react to what Brave yells,* he ordered himself. Had Cavatar's heart been knocked out? No, he seemed to be moving well enough. Once again Corgan tried to go after Brave's head, and this time the hit scored big. He took out one of Brave's eyes, and the monstrous Brave couldn't scream because a second punch tore out his throat.

Now Corgan blocked out everything except the need to fight. He didn't feel the bands that strapped him to his chair, didn't hear the yells of the crowd, didn't care about checking the scoreboard. He could feel his blood pumping with the desire to destroy Brave, could feel the neurons in his brain throb with impulses he channeled into waves so strong Cavatar surged forward, his fists pounding. And after eight and a half minutes Brave was beginning to fumble. His blows still landed, but Cavatar was making more hits.

Then Corgan misjudged and Brave knocked off one of Cavatar's hands. Corgan wasn't too worried; Cavatar could hit with his other hand, which he did, blinding Brave in his remaining eye. But Brave still didn't quit. He stood toeing the line, swinging wild punches so fast that Cavatar had trouble getting past those massive arms. Corgan wanted to get to the brain, to wipe out every section of Brave's skull the brain might lurk behind. When Corgan's Cavatar lost both feet, he balanced on the stumps of his ankles and swung upward from beneath Brave's pivoting arms. Luckily, Corgan couldn't feel his avatar's pain.

Next Brave gave a kick and sheared off the top of Cavatar's head. Corgan panicked! *"If you don't lose your head . . ."* Another split-second glance at the scoreboard showed that Cavatar had lost only one part of the left lobe of his brain. Could Cavatar still fight? He had three quarters of his brain left and an eye that could see Brave's ravaged face. He landed four more punches to Brave's head. That did it. Brave fell to the floor, where Cavatar pounded him again and again with his one remaining fist until only a few random pieces of Brave were left—one hand, one thigh, an elbow, and a piece of his heart. Brave was dead.

Instantly the chair straps sprang open. Corgan could stand. Bewildered by the roar of the crowd—were they cheering for *him*?—he just stood there. Suddenly a man rushed forward and grabbed him, pulling him to the center of the arena, where he raised Corgan's hand high. The cheers grew louder.

"Who are you?" Corgan asked the man.

"It's me, Thebos," he answered. "I got Lockered so I could get you out of here fast if you lost. I'll explain later."

So many shocks, one after the other! Corgan would never have recognized Thebos. He had a full head of curly brown hair and eyes that gleamed with energy. His skin was as taut as his muscles.

"How old are you?" Corgan asked in awe.

"Thirty. But look at the crowd, Corgan! They're cheering for you. You won!" Lofting Corgan's wrist, Thebos cried, "Folks, let's show our appreciation for Corgan here. The hero of the first Virtual War is once again a hero—of our own virtual war."

This time the roar was deafening.

Brigand would have slumped in defeat, except that his head was still strapped to the back of his chair. His face showed fury and hatred as Sharla, Cyborg, and Ananda rushed to Corgan, hugging him, slapping his back, congratulating him. Corgan's brain was still spinning when Thebos nudged him and told him, "You need to say something to these people. They want to hear your voice, Corgan."

As the visualizer lens trained on Corgan, the crowd's noise tapered off in anticipation. "I just want to say . . . ," Corgan began. "I mean . . . maybe now the Flor-DC can be returned to the citizens," he shouted. "There's a brilliant man here who can clean up the city and make your lives better again. He's right here—Mr. P. T. Thebos." This time it was Corgan who raised Thebos's arm in triumph, and the cheers doubled in volume. "And Ananda is your star, citizens," Corgan shouted. "Welcome her home to the Flor-DC."

Ananda pumped her own fists in a gesture of celebration, turning from side to side, nodding and smiling like the champion she was. Not wanting to intrude on Ananda's moment, Sharla and Cyborg stepped back, but Corgan couldn't keep his eyes off Thebos. He'd seen Sharla Lockered, and Cyborg and Delphine, but the transformation of that ninety-one-year-old elder into this young, supple, quick-moving, quick-talking man was phenomenal.

"*Nan*-da, *Nan*-da, *Nan*-da," the crowd kept chanting, but Ananda said, "Corgan, this is your party, not mine." When she raised her hands for quiet, the chanting died down, except for one high, shrill female voice that rang out from the crowd.

"What's your Instrument of Fate, Corgan? What'll you do to Brigand?"

"I don't—," Corgan started to say, but Thebos muttered, "Stop! Don't try to answer."

"Uh . . . I'll be choosing that tonight," Corgan told the crowd.

Then another loud voice shouted, "Show us Brigand's Instrument of Fate. What was he going to do to you?"

Corgan looked around at his friends, then told Ananda,

"You go ahead," and she strode across the square to the tall, shrouded object. When she took the cloth in her hand, the crowd grew so hushed Corgan could hear a baby whimpering. With a somber expression Ananda pulled off the cloth to reveal . . . a guillotine!

"He was going to cut off my head!" Corgan gasped as, behind him, Sharla let out a cry of horror. *The dream!* Once again Royal's grandfather's words rang in Corgan's head, this time in a different pattern. *If you* don't *win, you'll lose your head.*

Corgan felt an icy shock creep up his spine, and in that second he became a believer.

Twenty-one

Sharla was crying, her arms wrapped tightly around Corgan's neck. "Brigand really planned to kill you!" she wept. "I thought he was just messing with your mind, messing with all of us, but he meant it. You were right . . . and Thebos was right. . . ."

Though he tried to comfort her, Corgan felt pretty shaken too. "Can we end this now?" he asked Thebos and Cyborg. He wasn't used to standing up before throngs of people and trying to think of what to say, and he wanted to be alone with Sharla.

"It's up to you," Thebos answered.

Cyborg said, "You're the winner, Corgan. You get to make the rules, at least for today." Cyborg seemed as unnerved as the rest of them by the grisly instrument of death that stood nearby, seeming to loom more massive than it actually was.

"What do you want to do with Brigand?" Thebos asked. "Should we put him in the cell where you were?"

"Yes, but be sure to disconnect the mechanism that lets the cell's wall dissolve. I don't want Brigand to get out," Corgan said.

At Corgan's signal troopers released Brigand from the heavy chair. Brigand stood and straightened himself to his full height, then raised his chin and stomped through the square as if he were leading the troopers rather than being led, as though he were the victor rather than the defeated. "Don't let him get away," Corgan shouted. "Hold him! Tie his hands." Brigand threw a look not just of contempt, but of pure hatred toward Corgan and the friends around him.

Some of the citizens started to leave the city square, until Corgan said, "Let's go, Sharla," and took her hand to lead her away.

Then, in a rush, a few dozen people surged forward. In the same way they'd chanted for Ananda they began to yell, "*Cor*-gan, *Cor*-gan, *Cor*-gan," wanting to reach out and touch the new celebrity.

"Run!" Corgan yelled to Sharla, and they did, all the way to the medical center, where Corgan slapped his palm into the DNA identifier to force open the door. They barely got in before the herd of admirers stampeded outside the center, pounding on the door. "That was close," Corgan gasped. "I don't like this hero stuff."

Inside, Corgan and Sharla were surrounded again, this time by the members of the Robotic Nurse Corps. "We watched everything!" Nurse Eleven proclaimed in a voice that bubbled with enthusiasm, totally unlike the bland, controlled tone the robotic nurses usually used. "Congratulations, Corgan!" And then Eleven proudly added, "*I* was the one who took care of Corgan after his drowning when he first came to the Flor-DC."

"That's right, Eleven. You're the one who zapped me with an arc gun when I tried to get out." Eleven's humanlike face blushed a pale pink until Corgan said, "But I forgive you, Eleven. I deserved it."

Right then the door swung open and slammed shut immediately as Thebos ducked inside—the new Thebos, whose appearance was still so startling that Corgan's brain needed a quarter of a second longer than normal to process it.

"Wow!" Thebos exclaimed. "People are so celebrity obsessed! Maybe you should hide out here in the center for a couple of days till the furor dies down."

"Yeah, maybe, but listen, Thebos," Corgan began, "we hardly had a chance to talk out there, and I really want to hear about your Lockering. When did you do it, why did you do it, why did you choose thirty years old—the whole story."

"You mean right now?" Thebos asked. "With all your fans battering the door?"

"Yeah, sure, we can talk now, you and me and Sharla, too. Eleven, can you give us an empty room? And keep it private?"

"Gladly." Spinning on her wheels, Eleven rolled along the hall to the room where Cyborg had recuperated from the crash into the Atlantic. She opened the door and said, "I'll allow no one else to come in. If anyone tries to, I'll zap them with that same arc gun." Was that a little robotic humor? Corgan chuckled.

As Corgan and Sharla sat on the edge of the hospital bed and Thebos pulled up a stool to face them, Corgan's eyes scanned this room he remembered so well—the stark whiteness of the walls, the intercom voices that had seemed to come out of nowhere, the feeling of isolation.

"So!" Thebos began. "You want the whole story? Here it is. About two hours ago I found out that Brigand planned to guillotine you if he won the face-off. One of the troopers, who is a decent guy, slipped the information to me. Right away I tried to figure out my options. Dismantle the guillotine? Couldn't do that because it was guarded by half a dozen troopers."

Thebos ran a hand through that thick, curly brown hair that Corgan wasn't used to—and neither was Thebos, perhaps, because he kept touching it. "The smartest option would have been to get you out of your cell and manage an escape," he said. "But I made a stupid mistake. I mentioned that to Cyborg, forgetting that Brigand clues in to everything Cyborg hears. The next thing I knew, seven hulky troopers burst into my quarters and told me I was under arrest."

Sharla broke in, "I was there in the room when the troopers came and so was Cyborg. Three of the thugs made us leave and marched us over to the arena. They told us we had to stand on that white line till the face-off started. But . . . tell me what happened to you after we left, Thebos."

"Well, fortunately the troopers hadn't tied me up," Thebos continued. "They just locked me in and left me there. I was all alone in my quarters—with the Locker! And of course the troopers had no clue what the Locker was, if they'd even noticed it when they were there. It took me less than a minute to get it in working shape again. I'm an engineer extraordinaire, remember?"

"I remember." Corgan had once studied the blueprints for the *Prometheus*, the most amazingly designed flying vehicle ever built. Thebos was a creative genius, for sure, maybe the greatest that had ever lived.

Looking intently at Corgan, Thebos told him, "I knew I had to save you if you lost the challenge. But how? There I was, a doddering ninety-one-year-old, too feeble to knock down the door and fight the guards. And even if I did escape, I'd be noticed right away because everyone in the city would recognize me. Unless I became invisible . . ."

"Invisible!" Corgan gasped.

Thebos had begun to grin. "So then I thought, what better way to become invisible here in the Flor-DC than to shave sixty years off my appearance? Nobody would recognize me. I'd already figured out the way the Locker worked and that I could trigger it from inside."

"You Lockered *yourself*?"

"How am I going to tell this story if you guys keep interrupting?" But Thebos was laughing now. "So I went into the Locker as an old fool, and I came out as a . . . well, what you see here. Next I pulled the pillow-covered-by-a-blanket trick to make it look like I was in bed. Then I pounded on the door and told the guards that they'd locked me in the room by mistake, along with the old man, and I pointed to the bed. Of course the guards didn't recognize the new young Thebos, so they let me out." Thebos laughed even harder. "And then . . . they apologized for locking me in!"

"Holy . . . !" Corgan blurted out. "I can hardly believe it."

"Pretty amazing, huh?" Thebos agreed.

"But," Sharla began, "Corgan won the fight, so he didn't need you to rescue him after all. It was a matter of chance, wasn't it? Delphine talked about chance; she said other words for it were 'fortuity,' 'accident,' and 'fortune.'"

The amusement faded from Thebos's face. "You're right," he murmured, serious now. "I took a chance because I wanted to rescue Corgan, but that turned out to be unnecessary. And here I am young again, without a reason for being that way. I guess I'll have to find a new purpose for my life." In the quiet moment that followed, the three of them looked at one another, their expressions showing relief that things had turned out so well, but uncertainty about this pivotal point in their lives. Thebos stood up then and said, "I should go find Cyborg and Ananda and tell them how this all happened too. They didn't get a chance to hear the whole story. Do you two want to come with me? Or . . ."

"No," Corgan and Sharla both replied in the same breath. "We'll stay here for a while," Corgan added.

After the door had closed behind Thebos, Corgan asked, "Can you believe it? What a guy! Do you think he's sorry he's young now?"

"Why would he be? He's going to live forever," Sharla answered.

Corgan nodded. "And so are you, Sharla. But once, in this very room where we are now, I thought you weren't going to live at all. This is where they brought you after the Harrier crashed," he told her. "They put you onto this bed right here. You were all pale and bloody, and the robotic nurses said you might die. I was so scared!"

Sharla took his hand and said, "When I saw that guillotine today, I was terrified that you could have died too, Corgan. I don't ever want to lose you."

For a moment he was silent. Then, pressing her hand, he asked, "Does that mean it's you and me now? No more Brigand?"

As Sharla moved closer to him, she raised her face, her blue eyes steady on his. "Brigand lost me a long time ago, back in the Wyo-DC when he executed the members of the

Wyo Supreme Council. He said They were bad people, but that wasn't true. You and I knew Them, Corgan—maybe They didn't care enough about the citizens, but They weren't cruel. Just thoughtless."

"Wait. Back up. To the first part of that, the part about Brigand losing you a long time ago." All those months Corgan had been longing for Sharla, believing she was committed to Brigand—but she really wasn't? "Why didn't you tell me?"

Seeing the uncertainty on his face, she answered, "I just . . . wasn't ready. Right from the beginning I've known you're going to be a great leader. Maybe I've been afraid that if I got too close to you, I'd lose my identity. I want to be my own person, Corgan. I've always made my own choices and I always will. You're strong and you're growing stronger, and now you're a hero again. It's just . . . I don't want to fade into the shadows if I stand beside you. I guess that sounds selfish—"

"No, it doesn't, and you won't fade. How could you? You're pure gold," he said, holding her tightly.

"Pure." She smiled at him. "You were always worried about that, too, but it's true. And I know now that we'll be good together, because with you I can be stronger than I am if I'm alone." Her face was so close that the kiss was only millimeters away.

"Hold that thought," he said, pulling back just a little. "Eleven!" he shouted to the ceiling. "Turn off every monitoring device in this room, hear? Both visual and audio. I don't want anyone spying on us, no robots and no humans. And turn off all the lights in here—we don't need them."

The room became dim, then dark, then totally black. "Okay, now!" Corgan said.

He was the world's greatest controller of time, able to divide it into microseconds, but for the next while, time stopped as he shared with Sharla all his hopes and ambitions for their lives, now that he still had a life. When at last he opened the door to peer into the hall, the light blinded him a bit. Taking Sharla's hand, he said, "Let's go to Thebos's quarters. Everyone ought to be there by now. I think they'll be glad to see us."

Twenty-two

Corgan and Sharla heard music. The closer they got, the louder the music boomed, and when they threw open the door, they found a party in full swing, literally, with Thebos, Ananda, and Cyborg dancing around the room. "Like this!" Thebos was shouting as, with arms straight out, he bounced on one foot and pivoted around, holding his other leg hip-high. Where once his clothes had hung loose on his frail body, they now strained tightly across his shoulders, chest, and thighs.

"Here are the young lovers," Thebos shouted out.

"We were just talking, that's all," Corgan said, smiling. "You know, like conversation."

"Yeah. Sure." Thebos chuckled.

But it was true. In the darkness of that medical room Corgan and Sharla had talked and planned and decided what should be done, where they should go, what they could contribute to their world. Without a pause in his wild twirling Thebos cried, "Corgan and Sharla, come over here and form a circle with us. I'm teaching everyone to dance Greek."

They clasped hands with the others and scrambled to follow Thebos's instructions. "The music sounds a little bit like music from India," Ananda mentioned, laughing. "My grandma called it *bhangra*."

"This is pure Greek," Thebos assured her, panting a little. "All together now—boy, girl, boy, girl. Stay in a circle and watch my feet—step, step, step, skip a little, take another step forward, step back, hold one another's hands and hold them up high. It's how we used to dance at Greek weddings. I haven't danced in fifty years—it feels so good! *Hopa!*"

Even Corgan, who didn't much like dancing, got caught up in the joy of the moment. It had been a wild day: whipping Brigand at the challenge, seeing the guillotine that Brigand had had in store for him, but most important, knowing at last that Sharla loved him. So he stomped and kicked and yelled "*Hopa!*" every time Thebos did, even though he had no idea what *hopa* meant. Except that it must be Greek. Like Thebos.

When at last they were all winded, Thebos turned off the Greek music and they sank to the floor, still in a circle. Smiling, they congratulated one another, because each one of them had played a big part in the day's success. "Hey, I never knew," Corgan asked, "what did Cavatar look like?"

"I'll show you." With a wave of his hand Thebos illuminated the walls, those same walls that had once been covered with equations about thrust and propellant and zero gravity. And there, looming over all of them, was Cavatar.

Corgan studied his alter ego. Cavatar was nowhere near as ugly as Brave had been. He looked just as big, but the hair on his head was short and black, and his skin was tan, not meat colored. "Who designed him?" Corgan asked.

"I did," Sharla answered, settling against his chest. "Thebos designed Brave."

"Well," Thebos began, "take a look at us now. Here we

are, all together, and Brigand is in the cooler. I think it's time for you to tell us, Corgan, what his fate will be."

Corgan gazed around at the circle of his friends, the best and only friends he'd ever had in his whole life. But he shook his head. "You'll find out in the morning, which is now about nine hours, thirteen minutes, and twenty-seven and three hundredths of a second in the future, or at least it was when I started this sentence. Let's talk about anything else."

After an awkward silence Ananda suggested, "Like our plans. We'll talk about our plans and tell what we're going to do now." She linked her fingers into Cyborg's, smiling up at him.

"Well, first," Cyborg announced, smiling back at her, "Ananda's going to be a mother."

"What!" Corgan straightened up so fast he made Sharla's head bounce.

Ananda giggled. "He's talking about the puppies. In a few weeks Diva will have Demi's puppies, or clones, I should call them. And I decided I'm not going to get Lockered until I'm at least eighteen so I can try to catch up a little bit to Cyborg's mental acuity. There! Did I use that word right? 'Acuity'?" she asked Cyborg.

"You're learning." He pulled her against him.

It was a loving circle: Cyborg and Ananda, Corgan and Sharla; only Thebos sat alone, probably thinking about Jane Driscoll up there in the space station with her husband and son. "What about you, Thebos?" Cyborg asked.

"Personally?" Thebos shrugged. "I haven't had a personal life for so long I'll have to ease into it. But other things first," he answered. "If I'm going to live forever, I'll have a long time to work on Earth's problems. I'd like to restore radio

213

communication so we don't have to rely on fiber-optic cables, which break down too often. Then I'd like to work on cleaning the atmosphere so people don't have to be confined to domed cities. I mean, look at Nuku Hiva. Why is the air breathable there but nowhere else? I'd like to go there and find out."

Corgan got an image in his mind of Thebos meeting Delphine. What an interesting possibility that could turn into—Delphine and Thebos, those two brilliant scientists staying young forever, while Royal grew old by choice.

"But even before that," Thebos continued, "we have to restore reasonable governance to this city. Who's with me on that?"

"Ananda and I are," Cyborg answered. "We'll work with you."

"Excellent. And also I want to build that new zero-gravity spaceship. *Prometheus Two*. If the three of us—Cyborg and Ananda and I—gain enough influence in the new Flor-DC government, we'll persuade the citizens to make retractable doors in the dome, like in the Wyo-DC. That way I can launch *Prometheus Two*."

A second spaceship? "Why do you need another *Prometheus*?" Corgan asked, his hopes rising. "The first one still flies."

"Let me answer that with another question," Thebos said. "What are your plans, Corgan? And I assume they include Sharla."

Everyone turned toward them, waiting for their answer. Corgan inhaled, then said softly, "We'd like to go back to the Wyo-DC. That was our home. The New Rebel Troops have probably wrecked things there by now. Maybe if we go back, we can help put the place together again."

Before Corgan had finished, Thebos began to nod. "Somehow I figured that was what you'd want. That's why I plan to build *Prometheus Two*, so you can have *Prometheus One*. It's yours, Corgan. Yours and Sharla's. You can fly it back to Wyoming any time you want."

Elated, Corgan and Sharla hugged each other, and after that there was a lot of group hugging. Then Corgan suggested that everyone get some sleep, because tomorrow would be a mind-busting day. Instead of moving into separate rooms, they all arranged themselves on the floor of Thebos's quarters. Blankets weren't necessary; they kept one another warm.

Corgan actually slept. Maybe it was sensing Sharla near him, maybe it was knowing she would go with him to the Wyo-DC, maybe it was feeling like a hero again. For the first time in many nights his sleep was dreamless. And then, before he was ready, morning arrived.

"Time to proceed with Brigand's fate?" Thebos asked, glancing around the room. All of them sat up quickly, rubbing sleep from their eyes but very alert.

"Where is . . . ?" Corgan asked.

Thebos seemed to know what he meant. "I had it moved into one of the medical rooms."

"Right. First, have the guards bring Brigand here to your quarters, Thebos. If Brigand has anything to say before I create his fate, I want everyone to hear it."

Corgan didn't feel too nervous, which made him think that what he was planning was the right thing to do. The others stayed very quiet, especially Cyborg, who looked pale and tousled. Ananda reached up to smooth his wild red hair.

Not long afterward the door flew open and Brigand filled the doorframe. From behind, two unfamiliar guards pushed Brigand into the room so hard he stumbled, falling onto one knee right in front of Corgan. Glaring up, he snarled, "I'm not down here begging for mercy. This stupid artificial knee gave out. It's a piece of crap, just like Thebos is a piece of crap. Where is that freaky old geek? Did he die finally?"

"Oh, he's probably around somewhere," Thebos answered. Since Brigand didn't recognize him, the irony was wasted.

"Wait outside the door," Corgan told the guards, and closed it in their faces. "Brigand," he said, looking down at him, "you should say good-bye to all these good people because you won't have another chance to."

"You're going to kill me?" he sneered. "Corgan the avenger is going to destroy Brigand?"

Corgan answered sharply, "I just want you to say your good-byes while you can."

Brigand stared around him, hostility on his face. "There's no one in this room I care squat about," he declared. "Do your dirty deed, Corgan, whatever it is. You're a sniveling little failure. You won that face-off only because I let you."

"As if I believe that," Corgan answered.

Brigand taunted, "It's nice you decided not to kill me until this morning. I've had a whole night to mess with your mama."

"I don't have a mama," Corgan told him, anxious to end this waste of time.

Still on his knees, Brigand looked amused as he said,

"Sure you do. The mama who raised you, the one that turned from a mama into a papa when you were bad. Mama, papa—who knows what gender Mendor is, but whatever, I played with it."

Even kneeling in defeat Brigand managed to arouse anger in Corgan, who felt ready to lash out and hit him. But Cyborg broke in, "If you want to look at it that way, then Mendor is my mama too, Brigand. Mendor raised me when I was a little kid back on Nuku Hiva."

"Right, bro. That's how I managed to crash into the program. Your iris identification is still in Mendor's memory, and my iris ID is identical to yours." Brigand laughed, defying them all.

It wouldn't matter if Brigand had disabled Mendor's program, Corgan thought. The Mendor in the cell was just a copycat program of the original Mendor still in Corgan's old virtual-reality Box in the Wyo-DC. But Brigand went on, "So revenge will be mine—as someone said somewhere, sometime. Just wait!"

Empty threats. Brigand was powerless. "Come on, it's time to go," Corgan told him. He yanked Brigand to his feet, announcing, "I'm doing this alone. Just me and Brigand." Shoving him to the door, he turned to say, "The rest of you, please wait here and I'll call you when it's over." He left them standing wide-eyed and apprehensive in Thebos's quarters.

Four more New Rebel Troopers were waiting in the hall. Though yesterday they'd seemed loyal to Brigand, now they started pushing him around. "Stop that," Corgan ordered. "Just bring him into this room."

Inside, the troopers looked with interest at the object braced upright in the center of the room, but Brigand was busy announcing, "I suppose this is when I dispose of all my worldly goods. Ha! I don't have any worldly goods. Except this." He pulled off his shirt, probably because he wanted to show off his cannibal tattoos one last time. After rolling up the shirt, he handed it to one of the troopers, saying, "You can give this little memento to my trusted lieutenant. You know which one."

"Enough talk. Put him in here," Corgan said, indicating the Locker, "but keep holding him." After they'd forced Brigand inside, Corgan fastened the arm straps and then the metal helmet onto Brigand's head. "Now close the lid," he told the troopers.

"What is this thing?" one of them asked. "Are you going to electrocute him?"

"Just go," Corgan told them. "Shut the door on your way out."

Brigand must have heard the door slam shut. From inside the Locker his muffled voice rang out, "Screw you, Corgan!"

Funny, Corgan thought as he turned on the power. *That's what I said to him once.*

He'd worked out the dates in his head as closely as he could. As the whine of the motor crescendoed, he narrowed his eyes to stare at the dials. Then he threw the switch that turned on the program. The dates whizzed backward almost blindingly fast, just as they'd done for Delphine, for Sharla, for Cyborg, and presumably for Thebos. When the numbers on the dial spun to the date Corgan had chosen, he hit the red button.

Ignoring the screams that came from inside the Locker, he went to Thebos's quarters. "It's done," he told all of them. "You can come in now if you want."

In total silence they followed him to the room, where the screams had diminished to whimpers. "The Locker?" Sharla cried. "He's in the Locker?"

"You Lockered him?" Cyborg asked. "That means he's going to live forever!"

"Right." With hesitation Corgan touched the handle that opened the Locker. What would they think when they saw what he'd done to Brigand? He pulled open the door.

Ananda was the first to react. "Where is he?" she wanted to know, staring at eye level into the Locker. "He's not here!"

"Yes he is. Look down," Corgan answered.

The red-haired baby lay kicking and squirming at the bottom of the Locker, his face contorted with fury as he began to scream again.

"Is that Brigand?" Sharla gasped. "Yes, I can see . . . I remember how he looked when he . . . how old is he?"

"Six months. He'll live forever, but he'll never grow any older," Corgan told them as Cyborg dropped to his knees, staring speechless at his clone-twin, the infant Brigand.

"Why did you make him six months old, Corgan?" Thebos asked quietly.

"Because as an infant he can never hurt anyone again. He's trapped in a body that can't walk or talk."

They seemed stunned as they stared at the red-faced, screaming infant. "Even as a baby he was difficult," Sharla murmured uncertainly. "He demanded attention every minute."

No one looked happy. Maybe what Corgan had chosen for Brigand was too harsh, but it was all over now. His voice strained, he said, "Ananda, would you please call the robotic nurses to come and get this baby? He'll need to be taken care of—for the next hundred years and for eternity."

Twenty-three

Weeks later Ananda sat on the floor cuddling the two Demi clones. Just eight days earlier Sharla and Corgan, Ananda and Cyborg, had stood near the same spot, silent and attentive, distancing themselves a meter and a half from the surrogate mother, Diva, as she gave birth.

For Corgan it had been a miraculous moment. This was how ordinary life began in the real world of people and animals, so much more inspiring than the world Corgan had been born into, where babies got designed inside a test tube and were engineered for desired traits. That unnatural conception was how four of them had started out—Corgan, Sharla, Cyborg, and Brigand. And Brig, too, poor little brilliant Brig, whose flawed genetic engineering had condemned him to a short and painful life. The only one conceived and born naturally was Ananda.

These newborn puppies had been replicated—Delphine had cloned them from Demi—but they hadn't been altered at all from Demi, and the birth was real, two tiny bodies coming out of a living mother. As Diva licked the babies clean, rolling them around on their backs, their tiny squeals sparked emotions Corgan hadn't known he possessed: awe and respect for the beauty of life, along with wonder at the marvel of birth. Even though the newborns' wet coats lay flat against their tiny bodies, he could recognize Demi's markings: black hair all over except for white chests, white legs, and a band of white around their necks. Their muzzles were soft and pink almost all the way to the eyes. They reached out with stiff little legs, stretching their toes as though trying to touch this strange new world that they couldn't yet fathom because their eyes were still shut.

Now, eight days later, they lay nestled in Ananda's arms, still unable to see, but dry and soft and pretty. Diva watched from a box nearby, alert for any sounds or movement from the pups. She allowed no one but Ananda to touch them. As one of the pups yawned, curling its pink tongue, Corgan asked, "So, was it worth it, Ananda—all the trouble we went through to find Diva so she could have Demi's clones for you?"

Hesitant, Ananda answered, "I . . . can't tell for certain. I mean, I feel guilty for loving these precious little puppies as much as I do, because I think of my poor Demi up there in the space station with that weird Nathan, and I wonder if she misses me as much as I miss her. I don't want her to miss me—I want her to be happy, but . . . I'm mixed up about how I feel! Because these cloned puppies really are Demi. Aren't they?"

It was Sharla who went over and gave Ananda a hug, telling her, "It's all right to love the puppies. They're Demi clones, but they're themselves, and each one's a little different." And then, more softly, "It's possible to lose someone you loved, Ananda, and discover that you love someone else even more."

Those words sank into Corgan's consciousness like warm rain onto parched earth. He felt gratified because he knew the words were about him, and he wanted so much to accept them all the way. Maybe he would never be completely sure of Sharla, just as Ananda might always feel a bit of doubt about her love for the new dogs. Still, each of them had to be grateful for what was given to them, and build on it.

Cyborg turned from what he was doing to tell them, "I've sorted through Brigand's things, and take a look at what I found. He was keeping a Chronolog."

They gathered around the screen, with Ananda still holding the puppies. The lines on the screen read:

VIRTUAL WAR CHRONOLOG

The first terrorist attacks	Year 2001
The first plagues	2012
Eleven nuclear accidents	2012-2035
Nuclear wars begin	2038
Worldwide contamination; devastation complete	
Domed cities built to protect survivors	2038-2058

"I never knew he was doing this," Cyborg said. "I wonder when he started writing it."

"I wonder when he finished it," Ananda said. "Look at the next entry, Corgan. It says '2066, Corgan and Sharla are born.'"

The entries continued with a history of Brig's birth, their victory in the Virtual War, Corgan and Sharla's months on Nuku Hiva, and then it read:

2081 Sharla clones Brigand and Cyborg in her laboratory. She takes baby Cyborg to Nuku Hiva for Corgan to raise. Four months later, when the clone-twins are about eight years old, Cyborg nearly drowns, but

Brigand rescues him by cutting off Cyborg's hand, which was trapped beneath a boulder. *And that is the truth, I swear it! I swear!*

"So that *was* the way it happened, Corgan," Cyborg stated.

His cheeks burning, Corgan answered, "At least Brigand thought so." Had Corgan been wrong all along about the mutilation? He felt a sharp stab of uncertainty. If Brigand, for the noblest of reasons, had actually done what he said in the Chronolog—would it have changed anything? Not for Corgan. He and Brigand would have hated each other just as much, because both of them loved Sharla. But Corgan detested Brigand even more because he was evil incarnate, a treacherous bully who destroyed anyone that stood in his way.

The remainder of the Chronolog was about things that everyone knew: the Wyo-DC revolt, Corgan's escape in the Harrier, Brigand's crash through the dome, Sharla's brain injury. Brigand had even written about the voyage of the *Prometheus* to the space station, information he'd somehow managed to gather out of Cyborg's head while Cyborg was orbiting Earth.

They scanned the lines down to the last one. Brigand's final entry read, "Tomorrow I will execute Corgan."

That was it. No more. That final entry made Corgan feel justified that he'd Lockered Brigand—it was self-defense. At least Corgan hadn't murdered him. He never wanted to kill anyone, not ever, no matter what happened. He'd experienced war, and even though it was only a virtual war, the sights and sounds of suffering had cut into his conscience like exploding shrapnel.

It was Cyborg who brought up the question, one that had disturbed Corgan during several restless nights. "Thebos, can I ask you something?" Cyborg began. "When we were on Nuku Hiva, Delphine said she wasn't sure whether the Locker would wipe out a person's memories of things that had happened in their life before they got Lockered. Can you tell us? After you went back to thirty years old, did you forget what you learned between, say, age sixty and age ninety-one?"

Sharla added, "I've been wondering that too. I think all of us have."

"Mmm, it's hard for me to give you a definite answer," Thebos told them, speaking slowly as he glanced from one to the other. "Memory is so inexact, especially among old people. I'm not sure what was in my memory at different stages of my life, but I *have* noticed that I'm starting to remember things I haven't thought of for seventy years or more. Like songs lyrics from when I was in middle school."

Middle school? What was that? Corgan wondered. Before he could ask, Sharla raised a different question. "Thebos, please, can you tell us . . . what about Brigand? He's six months old now, but is it possible he remembers everything that happened in his whole life?"

Cyborg broke in, "Because that would be brutal. To have everything he ever learned and experienced stuck in his mind when he can't walk or talk or anything—that's cruel and unusual punishment! If his brain is still storing all of it, it'll be hell for him, because as a baby, he can't do anything. He's trapped! Helpless!" Cyborg shot a glance at Corgan, the person responsible for Brigand's fate.

"Wait now, wait!" Thebos raised his hand. "We need to

think about physiology and neurology. I can't speculate about Brigand, but I can tell you about my own reactions," he said as he slid quickly into lecture mode. "An old person's brain starts to get holes in it—I don't mean actual holes; I mean that the branches that are supposed to come out of the brain cells just aren't there any more. Aging had definitely impaired my ninety-one-year-old brain to a certain extent. Now I've gone back to a younger, more vibrant brain that lets me remember a lot more things, even if they're dumb things like song lyrics and dance steps from my teens. So what it comes down to is that I now have a more operable brain. As to how much I remember from before I was Lockered, I haven't figured that out yet."

Corgan's attention was riveted because he'd been trying to deal with some doubts of his own. Had his punishment for Brigand been—could it have been—too merciless?

"There's a huge difference between a baby's brain and an adult's brain," Thebos went on. "In brain size alone a baby obviously can't store as much information as an adult. So I really doubt that Brigand remembers his life before he was Lockered."

Corgan's sigh of relief was so audible that Sharla squeezed his hand.

"But . . . ," Cyborg stammered, "you're not sure."

"Can't be sure of anything, Cyborg," Thebos told him. "We just don't have enough data to come to any scientific conclusions." He paused, glanced down as though considering something, then told them, "I'm going to share with all of you what I've been tossing around in my own mind since I Lockered myself."

"Hold on just a minute." Ananda returned the puppies to

their mother and then joined the rest of them in the circle on the floor. They'd been spending a lot of time together in Thebos's quarters, learning from him while they enjoyed one another's company. It had become a habit for them to arrange themselves in the identical circle: Corgan, then Sharla next to Ananda, then Cyborg, and at the focal point of the perimeter, Thebos.

"Okay, here's what I've been considering," Thebos told them. "After we get the Flor-DC straightened out and running again, I'd like to do some reverse engineering on the Locker and find out if I can change its operation. The way it works now, when you're Lockered, you get frozen into one age forever. Maybe I can rework it so that after you get Lockered, you can go forward again if you want to and mature naturally from that age on."

Cyborg brightened. "Then Brigand could grow up to be a normal kid!"

No way on Earth, Corgan wanted to yell. It didn't matter what age Brigand might grow to, he'd always be a savage ready to annihilate anyone who opposed him. Corgan was about to say that when he looked up and saw the hope in Cyborg's eyes.

The words of protest died on Corgan's tongue. If Cyborg wanted to pretend that his clone-twin was redeemable, Corgan would not destroy the illusion. Instead he gave a little half nod in Cyborg's direction.

Turning away, he told himself that it was time to forget Brigand and concentrate on his own future. His and Sharla's.

He crossed the room to pick up the i-pen beside the screen, where Brigand's Chronolog still glowed. "August 15,

2082," he wrote. "Corgan and Sharla will fly the *Prometheus* to the Wyoming domed city."

Sharla smiled at him. Tugging at his fingers, she took the i-pen, leaned over the screen, and added, "Where they will remain happily ever after, except for a few tours through the universe."

That was it. The Virtual War Chronologs had ended. Now all of them would begin the task of rebuilding Earth, trying to help the human race grow strong again.

"Save this Chronolog," Corgan said to his friends. "The world needs to remember."

THE END